The
DISAPPEARING

OTHER BOOKS BY
JEFF VANOUDENHOVE

SERIES

THE DARK SERIES

Dark Place
Dark Lane
Dark Queen
Dark Child
The Final Dark

THE ALPHABET KILLER SERIES

The Alphabet Killer
The Letter Man
Killer by Number

STANDALONE NOVELS

Just Listen

Emma

Reaper House

SHORT STORY COLLECTION

Screams in the Dark and Other Twisted Tales

The DISAPPEARING

JEFF VANOUDENHOVE

JAVO
PUBLICATION

Westfield, MA

JAVO Publication
Westfield, Massachusetts 01085

ISBN: 979-8-9918888-7-5

Library of Congress Control Number: 2025928258

Cover design by Jeff VanOudenhove

To my faithful readers.
Thanks for making this a wonderful journey

Chapter 1

The sound of the squeaky shower knob turning the water off awakens me from a restful sleep. At least, it *feels* like the sleep was restful. I don't recall anxiously waking in the night, beating down my troubled thoughts, and the bed isn't in complete disarray like it has been these past few weeks. I've had a lot on my mind lately with the job hunting, the past-due bills, and of course, the little surprise that wasn't supposed to happen but did, and with it, more that we can't afford to care for properly. Today's adventure had better produce results, or we won't make it another month in this apartment. Our absentee landlord has already threatened eviction twice. Jason does what he can, but he can't support everything. He's already working more hours than he should, and my unemployment checks are laughable. I need to get this job. *We* need me to get this job.

I stay lying still, letting my thoughts wander, enjoying the comfort of the blanket I've cocooned myself in. *Don't get used to it, Marney; you'll have to start getting out of bed early again once you win over the folks at Tutter & Associates with your undeniable charm.*

I hear Jason rummaging through the vanity drawers as he does each morning, looking for tweezers, clippers, or some other self-grooming tool to pretty himself up. I swear, that man is worse than I am. Well, worse than I used to be when I had a reason to get ready in the morning. And I *will* have a reason again. But somehow, he'll still find a way to be more beautiful.

I smile and roll my eyes at the thought before glancing at the alarm clock on my nightstand. 6:22. I let out an exhausted sigh. Did I really want to go back to getting up this early? I'd gotten used to rolling over and going back to sleep, eventually crawling out of bed after the eight o'clock hour. No, darn it! I can't think that way. The interview is at 9:00. I can't afford to look groggy while trying to impress. But.., maybe just a few more minutes.

The bathroom door swings open, revealing Jason shirtless with only a towel wrapped around his waist. He hasn't completely dried himself, as stray beads of water trickle down his chiseled chest and stomach before absorbing into the towel. His dirty blonde hair is still damp, unbrushed, but swept back by his hand in such a way that still makes him look good without trying. Damn him! I have to work twice as hard to look half as good. It's the high cheekbones and valley-sized dimples, I tell myself. Some people are just born to be gorgeous. That's his curse. At least, I can always fall back on that one thought that keeps me smiling - *I'm hittin' that!*

He doesn't notice me staring at him as he stomps across the room to the tiny closet we share. We don't have much space or a lot of furniture, so we agreed to share half the closet and half the dresser. Somewhere in his head, that translated to half the closet and all but one drawer of the dresser. Since he does all the cooking, I didn't fuss over it. I don't mind that my clothes get stacked in folded piles on top of the dresser. It's not like I've needed them to look neat or wrinkle-free in over three months, anyway. However, if things go well today, I may have to reclaim a drawer or two.

As I watch Jason frantically sliding the hung shirts back and forth along the rod, I can't repress the feeling any longer and let out an audible yawn. The noise alerts him to my now conscious status, and he begins to rattle off questions.

"Do you know where my black shirt is, hon?" he asks without turning from the hanging clothes. "The one with the embroidered emblem on the pocket."

"You wore that on Monday," I reply.

"No, I didn't. I wore the navy blue polo with the paisley design on the front."

"That was Tuesday. Did you check the laundry basket?"

"I'm telling you, I didn't wear it. It should be here."

I sigh heavily and peel the blankets off me. I love the man to death, but he can't remember from one day to the next. It isn't his fault. He sustained a massive concussion in high school that left him with permanent brain damage, affecting his short-term memory. Some days are better than others. Some days are worse. I wonder if one day he'll forget about *me*. Who am I kidding? I'm downright unforgettable.

While he continues sorting through the hangers, I stride to the laundry basket and dig my hands in deep. What I'm looking for is near the bottom, but it's there, nonetheless. I pull the shirt from the pile and tap my foot playfully on the floor to gather his attention.

"Is this what you're looking for?" I ask, dangling the shirt from my fingertips and smiling.

He pauses what he's doing and pokes his head out from behind the door. When he sees the shirt he was anxiously searching for, he slumps his head.

"Did I really wear that on Monday?" he asks.

"You did."

"Shit! I like that one. I have to meet a supplier later today, and I wanted to look professional."

"Go with the dark green one," I say, pointing into the closet. "You look good in green."

"You think so?"

"Definitely."

"What about you?" he asks. "Are you feeling ready for your interview?"

"I'm fine. I'll do fine. I'm fine."

He shoots me a whimsical look, like my answer wasn't convincing enough. It wasn't, but I didn't expect him to pick up on that.

"You're going to be great," he assures me with his dimpled smile.

"How do you know that?"

His eyes shift downward to my stomach and then back up to meet mine. "Because we have faith in you."

I tilt my head sideways, flash a lighthearted grin, and roll my eyes.

"Lame."

Jason shrugs his shoulders, smiling, and drops his towel while reaching into the top dresser drawer for underwear. He's never been a bashful one. It took me a while to get used to his free-spirited nature. I was a bit uncomfortable in the beginning, the way he felt so at ease traipsing around naked without a care, while I squirreled myself away in the confines of the bathroom, even when only changing my shirt. Maybe if I had the toned body he has? Nope; I still don't think I'd flaunt it as much as he does. I'm way too self-conscious about the way I look.

"I'm going to hop in the shower. You'd better have saved me some hot water."

He doesn't respond, focusing more on which color of underwear to choose, as if his supplier will be inspecting to make sure the color scheme is favorable with the rest of his outfit. I close the bathroom door behind me, wondering if there's something wrong with me for not having that same level of commitment toward my wardrobe. I let out a silent giggle as I peer at my frumpy self in the mirror. My strawberry-blonde hair is scraggly and knotted, and apparently, running for dear life in all directions from my scalp. I lean in, looking at the smattering of light-colored freckles across my nose and upper cheeks, my pale complexion almost glowing under the lights. Whoever came up with "luck of the Irish" certainly wasn't referring to skin tone or sunburn susceptibility.

I turn the squeaky shower faucet on, letting the water heat up while I undress, looking away from the mirror for fear I might burn out my rods and cones from the extreme brightness. Casper the Friendly Ghost has more color than I do. I step under the warm water, close my eyes, and let the soothing liquid wash over me to calm my nerves while I wipe my hands across my face. When I reopen my eyes, I notice two words written in soap on the tile wall. It's something Jason has done every day for the past six weeks since I told him the news. Though partially washed away, this morning's "Good luck" message makes me smile. The warmth of his sweetness reinforces my belief that today is going to be a great day.

Chapter 2

The dripping was an annoyance. A slow, measured plink from the kitchen sink, steady as a metronome, that seemed to echo in my head long after I stopped hearing it. I'd asked the landlord about fixing it, but he blew it off, stating something about it being an old building. Everything in our lives felt like an old building—leaning, creaking, threatening to collapse in on itself.

I pour myself a cup of coffee and stare at my reflection in the microwave door. My face looks older than twenty-eight—shadows under the eyes, skin too pale. I almost don't recognize myself, but the glaring freckles give me away. I playfully stick my tongue out at myself to lighten my sour mood and decide it's only the tinted glass on the microwave door that is warping my reflection. See? I feel better already.

A few moments later, after downing my coffee like I'm a caffeine fanatic, I am out the door, dressed in my only decent blouse and the black skirt I keep promising to replace. I lock the apartment, double-check the knob, then hesitate in the hallway. Something strikes me about the door across from ours. Had it always been blue? No, last week it was beige. I'm sure of it. The neighbor of three years—a woman named Angie—used to hang a little wreath of fake flowers on it. She had a seven-year-old daughter who used to run up and down the hallway. But now, there was no wreath, and a nickel nameplate below the spy hole read "Larson." That was fast. I didn't hear anyone moving in. I shrug and shake it off. I don't have time to dwell on it. I have an employer to smooth-talk.

* * *

The dangling cow keychain holds my attention as I sit quietly in the parking lot of Tutter & Associates. I've arrived fifteen minutes early for my interview, but don't want to seem too anxious. For now, the cow keeps my thoughts preoccupied, with the words, "I love moo," coming from its mouth in a cartoon word balloon. Jason meant well when he bought it for me for my twenty-sixth birthday. At some point, I had told him I liked manatees. Jason looked at me, puzzled. I said, you know, sea cows. He thought a cow in the sea was the most hysterical thing ever. Since then, and with his memory issues, he only remembers cows and assumes they are my favorite animal. Nope. Not even close. Cows give me the creeps. I couldn't help but look surprised when I opened my gift. Admittedly, my reaction could have been better. I know Jason felt bad about his mistake. The good news is, with his brain injury, he didn't remember it by the next day. But the thought of Jason picturing cows in the ocean makes me chuckle, so I kept the keychain. Plus, the fake cow doesn't bother me as much as the real thing.

I take in a deep breath and let it out slowly, trying to brush away all the anxiety. I pull my visor down and look in the mirror to ensure I'm still presentable. I may have applied a bit too much color to my cheeks; it's still better than looking like paste. I push the visor back up, grab my keys from the ignition, and step from my car, ready to present to Tutter & Associates their newest and brightest hire. Fingers crossed, anyway.

As I walk by the front of my car, I cringe at my parking job, noticing that my front bumper is only an inch away from touching the concrete barrier at the base of a lamppost. My brain always jumps to worst-case scenarios, and it conjures up images of what the disaster would have looked like if I'd hit it. I would probably kiss the job goodbye from embarrassment alone, and I'd be looking at a hefty car expense to replace the bumper, which I wouldn't do, since we don't have the funds. I'd be stuck driving around with a dented bumper for all to see. *Look at me; I can't drive.* Let it go, Marney; you didn't hit it.

I walk toward the front entrance, admiring the company's logo above the door: an open ledger with a quill pen writing on the page. This company seems more professional than the previous places I've worked. Maybe they'll *act* more professionally, too. I step into the lobby, where I am greeted by an attractive woman seated behind a large, half-round desk.

"Hello. May I help you?"

"Yes, Hi. I have an interview at 9:00."

"Can I have your name, please?"

"Marney Leery," I offer reflexively. "I mean, *Fitzgerald*," I hastily correct myself. "Marney Fitzgerald."

The slender woman looks at me curiously.

"My maiden name," I tell her to appease her confusion.

She smiles and nods. "Just a moment, please. I'll let Mr. Tutter know you're here."

"Thank you."

I turn and see three cushioned leather chairs along the side wall and decide it's best to occupy one of them while I wait, instead of standing by the desk looking overly eager. I ease into the one closest to the windows; a faint smell of antiseptic wafts from it. The cushions are comfortable, and I imagine the accommodations for the employees are just as good, if not better. The lobby is open and bright, with windows along the front wall running from floor to ceiling. The furnishings are modern and neutral-colored. *Just park my desk out here, please; I'll be happy.*

I look down at the keys still in my hand and shake my head at my earlier response. *Marney Leery.* If only that were true. Jason wanted to wait to get married until our financial situation was better. I threatened him that he wasn't getting out of it, telling him I'd use his last name as a constant reminder. I should have known it would trip me up one of these days. I slide the keys into the front pocket of my purse just as the receptionist calls over to me.

"Mr. Tutter will see you now."

I stand as she points to a door to the right of her desk.

"Right through that door and to your left," she says, smiling.

"Thank you," I respond, finding it odd not to have a chaperone.

I open the door into a narrow hallway with cubicles ahead of me. To my left is an open door into what appears to be a small conference room. I see a white-haired man sitting at a large table, tapping the back of a pen against a notepad, and I surmise, based on the receptionist's instructions, that *that* is my destination. I step into the open doorway, mildly timid, and quietly announce my presence.

"Hello, I'm here to interview for the bookkeeper position."

The man stands from his chair. "Ms. Fitzgerald?"

"Yes."

"Hello, I'm Jedidiah Tutter." He extends his arm to a chair across from him. "Please, have a seat."

I thank him and sit down in the chair he assigned me. He sits, too, staring down at a copy of my resumé. After the initial greeting, he gets right down to business.

"I see it's been a few months since you were last employed," he opens with. "Was that a planned hiatus?"

"No," I answer. "It's been difficult finding a job. It seems employers are either looking for someone to work part-time or only temporarily. In my experience, I've noticed the full-time positions tend to go to those who are overqualified."

"How do you mean, 'overqualified'"?

"Well, I believe companies are looking for experienced, educated accountants who they can pay a bookkeeper's salary."

"Well, I assure you, Ms. Fitzgerald, we have our fill of accountants. What we need is a good bookkeeper – someone to keep our files and ledgers in order. Maybe some other odds and ends around the office. Looking at your work history, you seem to have a good level of experience."

"I do," I state confidently, nodding. "I'm good at my job. And I'm very serious about it."

He smiles at me. "I can tell." He looks down at my resumé and then raises his eyes so he is looking through his white, untrimmed, and untamed eyebrows. "Can you tell me why you are no longer with your previous employer?"

I feel my heart beating faster from his question. I don't know why I feel surprised; I knew there was a good possibility the subject would arise. I take a deep breath, let it out, then calmly speak.

"My previous boss thought it was acceptable to make sexual advances toward me. I told him I was uncomfortable with his actions, but he persisted. I called him a..," I hesitate, wondering if I've said too much. *You've come this far, Marney; don't stop now.* "I called him a perverted asshole and then quit."

"I see," he says, looking unfazed. "I appreciate your candor. It's refreshing. Most job applicants tell me what they think I want to hear."

"I've always been a straight-shooter, Mr. Tutter." *Straight-shooter? Where did that come from?*

"I understand," he responds. "You realize, Ms. Fitzgerald, if I were to offer you the position, you would be expected to come in on an occasional Saturday. Would that be a problem?"

I think about the wrinkles that situation would cause in my personal life, and then I think about how living on the street would cause an even bigger wrinkle if I don't get a job soon.

"It wouldn't be a problem at all," I answer.

"Well then, there's only one question left to ask. Can you start on Monday?"

"Monday?" I repeat, shocked. "Like, right after the weekend, Monday?"

"That would be the one, yes."

I picture my jaw open wide enough to catch flies as I sit speechless and dumbfounded.

"I apologize," Mr. Tutter continues. "Don't answer yet. How silly of me. We haven't even discussed salary or benefits. I'll tell you what – I'll have the receptionist make up a packet for you. Take it home, review it, and give me your answer tomorrow."

"I...I don't know what to say."

"Perhaps, by tomorrow, you will."

"Thank you," I say, standing from my chair and extending my hand. "Thank you so much, Mr. Tutter."

He stands and accepts my handshake. "Thank *you*, Ms. Fitzgerald, for being open and honest."

"I'll review the paperwork and have my answer for you in the morning."

"Very well."

I nod graciously and walk to the door to exit, but then stop. Guilt washes over me. Mr. Tutter said I was 'open and honest,' but I haven't been *entirely* open. I turn back to the stately gentleman.

"Mr. Tutter? I know I don't have to divulge this, but for the sake of honesty, I think it's only fair you should know. I'm six weeks pregnant. I'll understand if you..,"

The older man throws his hand up to stop me from continuing and smiles. "Review the packet, my dear. I'll await your answer tomorrow morning."

My shoulders drop four inches as the heavy weight I've been carrying slides from them. I return an appreciative smile.

"Thank you again," I say before stepping from the small conference room. After closing the door, I take a moment to lean back against its surface to gather myself. *I knew today was going to be different. I could feel it. Everything is falling into place. We're going to be all right.*

Chapter 3

I gather the benefits package from the recep-tionist and squeeze the manila envelope be-tween my upper arm and side ribs while I fumble for my keys. I'm feeling so pumped about the job that when I walk back into the parking lot, I can't contain my excitement. I immediately grab my phone and dial Jason to tell him the news. I'd forgotten he mentioned he'd be with a client until his phone kicks me to voicemail. I start to leave a message, "Jason, I have some great news..." and then lose track of my thoughts as I approach the lamppost where my vehicle was parked. My mind goes blank. I pull the phone from my ear and hit the end call button, as I glance around me in con-fusion. My car is not where I parked it, but instead, two parking spaces to the right of the lamppost.

Is my mind playing tricks on me? Didn't I park it here? I specifically recall how close I'd come to causing an embarrassing scene. I walk over to inspect the vehicle. I think it must belong to someone else, but then, where is my vehicle? I wasn't in a tow-away zone. I look through the driver's side window and spot the three pens I keep in the center console and the brown paper bag acting as a floor mat on the passenger side floor. It's my vehicle, for sure. I look behind me at where I thought I remembered parking my car and shrug my shoulders. *I'm losing it.* I walk around the vehicle, looking for dents and scratches as if believing someone must have taken it for a joyride while I was inside and then returned it to the wrong spot. I know that's not the case, but I do my exterior audit anyway. When I'm satisfied with its condition, I shake my head, thoroughly perplexed. I must have been confused.

I brush it off and hop into the driver's seat, slapping the benefits package down on the passenger seat. It's a twenty-minute drive back to the apartment, which will give me the rest of the day to review the details of my new job before Jason gets home. *My new job.* That sounds good. Unless there's something ridiculous with the benefits, that's what it will be. I tap the envelope with my fingers and whisper, "My new job." I smile, feeling giddy, then start the car and pull out of the parking lot.

I'm halfway home and feeling over the moon when my car suddenly starts to jerk, and the engine begins randomly revving, slowing down, and speeding up. The red check engine light kicks on. My thoughts shift back to the parking lot and how my car was misplaced. *I knew it; someone messed with my car.*

I begin to panic, less about the car trouble or what someone might have done to it, and more about how much it will cost to fix it. And how will I get to work if the car breaks down? Luckily, there is an Auto Service Center on this stretch of road. It's about a mile from my current location. I only hope my car can squeak it out.

I realize how bad my sense of distance is when, a harrowing three miles later, I'm barely rolling into the garage parking lot. I pull into the first available spot, where the engine revs its discontent before sputtering and stalling. I let out a heavy breath, relieved it waited to conk out until I was at the garage.

I step from my vehicle and make my way into the lobby, the smell of rubber and oil thick in the air. A young man behind the counter, maybe in his mid-twenties, asks if he can help me. I step forward, glancing at the name patch above his shirt pocket, the name Freddie embroidered in white lettering. I am at once comforted, reminded of my Uncle Freddie, whose house on the Cape we would visit every year when I was a little girl.

"Hi. My car just started acting up on my drive home. I barely made it here."

"Can you tell me what the issue is?" he asks.

"I don't really know. It was driving fine, and then it started shuddering and slowing down. Then it would jump forward suddenly, rev up, before slowing down again. The engine light went on. I think somebody did something to it."

"I don't know anything about that," he says, checking off boxes on a form, "but it sounds like it might be your transmission." He looks behind him at a calendar on the wall before turning back to face me. "We're all booked today, but I can squeeze you in tomorrow morning if you'd like."

"I don't think I have much choice," I tell him. "I think it died out front."

He leans sideways to look around my shoulder out the front window. "Oh. Well, unfortunately, we don't offer rentals. Do you have someone who can give you a ride?"

"It's not a big deal; I can call for an Uber." *Another expense we can't afford.*

"Okay," he says. "Let me get all your information down and get the keys from you. We'll take a look at it tomorrow and figure out what the problem is."

I thank the young man and offer up my information and my keys. I make my way to a little waiting area, where I call for an Uber. I try desperately not to think about how much the car repair will cost since the new job will help financially. That thought reminds me that I still have the paperwork in the car. The wait will give me a chance to look over the benefits. At the very least, maybe it will help put me in a better mood.

I run out and grab the envelope from the passenger seat, quickly looking around to see if there is anything else I need to take with me. Once I'm satisfied with my brief inspection, I head back into the waiting area. The Uber app shows my ride will be here in twelve minutes. I settle into the molded plastic chair, about to dig into the envelope, when an uncontrollable itch comes upon the underside of my right arm. I reach to scratch it and immediately wince at how tender the spot is to the touch. I twist my arm up and notice three dark bruises beside each other in a straight line, each about the size of a dime. *Where the hell did those come from?*

I try to recall the previous night's activities and the earlier hours of my morning, hoping something will jump out at me as to the cause of the bruises, but nothing comes to mind. I gently rub my fingers along the skin's surface as if I'm a masochist, feeding off the pain. I place the first three fingers of my left hand onto each of the darkened spots, noticing how perfectly they fit, almost as if the marks had been formed by someone who had forcibly grabbed me. *That didn't happen; I would have remembered something like that.* I scan the rest of my arm, looking for other blemishes, but find none. Shaking my head, I pass it off as another one of life's great mysteries.

I again reach for the benefits package just as a car's horn sounds, notifying me of my ride. I look at my phone. *Three minutes early. Someone will be expecting a bigger tip.*

I walk to the exit to notify the driver I'll be right out. I turn and see Freddie focused on a computer monitor. I call out to him to get his attention.

"So, I'll hear from you tomorrow sometime?"

"Sure will," he replies. "Someone will give you a call once we determine what's going on with the vehicle."

"Okay, thank you."

I walk out to catch my ride, feeling a little better. It's only Wednesday, so I still have time to get the car back before Monday, if I decide to accept the position. With what the bill is going to cost me, I feel obligated. Either take the job and survive a bit longer, or get tossed out on the street. Not much of a decision.

Chapter 4

Going through the paperwork is rather exciting. The salary is more than I've made at any previous job. I did a quick Google search and found that the pay is actually a bit higher than the industry standard for a bookkeeper position. That alone is almost enough reason to accept the offer. The health benefits are also quite reasonable, but I'll have to compare with Jason's to know for sure. Employees get two weeks of vacation each of the first two years, after which it increases to three weeks. They also get forty hours of sick time and ten paid holidays. There is also a 401K plan I can sign up for. I quickly skim through the middle section of the pamphlet regarding pet insurance and a mental healthcare support hotline. That doesn't pertain to me. Then, I get to the segment I am most curious about. The company allows twelve weeks of paid maternity leave.

Everything seems fantastic. I can't wait to tell Jason. I look at my phone and see it's already 4:30. I decide it's time to get off my butt to do something around the apartment. Since I haven't been working, I've gotten used to having the place in tip-top shape by the time Jason gets home. I know he's gotten used to it, too. I wonder how disappointed he'll be when that changes.

While doing the dishes, an idea comes to mind. I've never been much of a cook, but it would be a nice gesture to have dinner ready when Jason arrives. He's been working so much lately, and I feel I haven't contributed much. I can't make anything extravagant, but I think we have a can of Sloppy Joe sauce I can work with.

I start browning the ground beef and let my thoughts wander. Twelve weeks of maternity leave. I don't recall Jason's work having a similar policy for fathers, though it would be nice to have him home for some of that time. Maybe they have a shorter two or four-week unpaid leave. Can we afford that? I'll ask him how much vacation time he has saved up. That will help.

My thoughts get interrupted by the ringing of my phone. It's Jason. His ears must have been burning. *That's only when you're speaking about someone, dummy.*

"Hey, hon, I was just thinking about you," I tell him. "Oh, nothing important. But I do have exciting news to share. What? Oh, really? No, that's okay. Don't worry; I'll figure something out. Of course, it's fine. Do what you need to do. My news? It's nothing. It can wait until you get home. Okay. Love you, too. Bye."

Well, that just figures. The one time I decide to surprise Jason with dinner, he gets invited out to a fancy restaurant with his boss and the new supplier they've been trying to win over. I look down at the simmering meat and crinkle my nose. *Cheap date for one, please.*

I finish my gourmet meal, pack away leftovers, do the dishes, and settle into the couch for a movie. I scan through the different channels on my streaming service until I land on something that looks like it might hold my attention. It does the trick for about an hour before I feel my eyelids getting heavy. I lean sideways toward the sofa arm to rest my head on the pillow for a moment. Before I know it..,

My eyes shoot open at the sound of my phone ringing. It doesn't immediately register that I'm in bed until I reach for my phone on my nightstand.

"Hello? Yes, speaking. I'm sorry, who is this? Oh, right; my car." The reminder makes me notice the hint of light coming in from behind the closed curtains. It's morning. "What's the damage?" I question, expecting bad news. "Oh, really? That's great! Yes, thank you. Go ahead. Okay, I'll see you then. Bye."

I hang up and slump my head to my chest in relief. It wasn't my transmission, after all. It was a serpentine belt. Freddie from the service center said they could have it in and out before 11:00. I look to my left to see that Jason isn't in bed. I hold my phone up and squint until the blurriness fades enough for me to tell the time. It's 8:37. Shit. Did I really sleep through Jason getting ready for work? I must have been exhausted. I don't even remember dragging myself to bed last night.

I spin sideways and plant my feet on the floor while letting out a yawn. Rubbing my hand down my face, I feel disappointed that I didn't get to tell Jason about my interview. I stand and walk to the window, peeling open the curtains to let in some light, then drag myself into the kitchen to start the coffeemaker before making my way to the bathroom for my waking shower. When I undress, I catch a glimpse of my arm in the mirror and notice the bruises I'd sustained have grown in size, enough to blend into one large blotch. I run my fingers over it again and clench my teeth, feeling the same tender soreness as I did the day before. *I wish I knew what I did.*

I shrug it off and run my hand under the bath spout, waiting for the water to get to a steamy temperature. Turning my head to the back of the shower wall, I see another soap message from Jason waiting for me. This one says, "Smile, babe." And I do. He can be a sweet man. I'm sorry I missed him this morning.

When the water reaches my desired temp, I step under the shower and let the stream wash over me like it's stripping away my old life to make way for a new, improved version. I think about the job opportunity offered to me and how I can't let my indecisiveness ruin a chance at a dream job. I didn't get to discuss things with Jason, but I'm going to accept the position. Mr. Tutter seems like he's a great employer, and more importantly, I need the job. I know Jason will be more than enthusiastic about it, and maybe a little relieved that he doesn't have to carry our financial burden alone.

After I've finished my daydreaming session and rinsed the remaining shampoo from my hair, I turn the water off and step out of the shower. The cool air invigorates me while I wrap the towel around myself. When I open the bathroom door, the inviting aroma of freshly brewed coffee stimulates my senses enough that I feel obligated to take a detour to the kitchen to pour myself a cup before I even think about getting dressed. I take my first sip, and it's so worth it. The soothing liquid comforts my soul, and I wonder if it tastes better this morning because of the offer of a new job or if I've finally figured out the correct measurement of grounds-per-cup ratio. I'm leaning toward the former but hoping for the latter. I could use this kind of Heaven each morning.

I take another sip, then rest my cup on the counter while I go to get ready. Looking at my wardrobe, it's clear that a portion of my first paycheck will be going toward some new clothes. If I'm going to be professional, I'll need to dress the part. And shoes! I'll need more shoes. There's no way I'm going to continue to let Jason win *that* race.

Slow down, girl. I've already spent my entire paycheck before I've even started the job. Keep focused. Necessities first. The car. I'm so relieved it wasn't something that would completely break the bank or force me into finding a new vehicle. We'd be digging ourselves out of a hole for months, trying to catch up. Freddie quoted me $347 for parts and labor. That's manageable. He said it was a good thing I was close to a garage, or I could have done some irreparable damage had I kept driving. Irreparable to my wallet, maybe.

I grab my phone and park myself on the couch, pulling up the number to Tutter & Associates. While the line rings, I smile at the idea that *I* will soon be one of those "associates." A woman answers; I picture her to be the same woman I met at the front desk.

"Hello, this is Marney Fitzgerald. I interviewed yesterday for the bookkeeper position. Is Mr. Tutter available? Yes, no problem."

She puts me on hold; the song Africa by Toto plays through the speaker. I find myself humming along to the tune and strangely hoping Mr. Tutter doesn't pick up until after the chorus. Unfortunately, my hopes are dashed, replaced with butterflies in my stomach as Mr. Tutter's voice rings out before the chorus hits.

"Hi, Mr. Tutter. It's Marney Fitzgerald. I'm calling to let you know I've decided to accept the position. Yes, that's right. No, thank *you* for the opportunity. I'm looking forward to it. Yes, will do. Monday at 8:00. See you then. Goodbye."

I hang up and let out an excited squeal. I did it! I'm officially employed again. I'm tingling from head to toe and can't keep myself from prancing around the living room in jubilation. The smile on my face must be so big it's causing permanent crease lines in my cheeks. I sprint back to my half-empty coffee cup and top it off with more deliciousness, thinking there's only one thing left that can make me feel even better than I already do. I pick up my phone, open the Spotify app, and begin playing Toto's Africa.

Chapter 5

I instructed the Uber driver to meet me out front; getting in and out of the rear parking lot can sometimes be challenging. While I wait on the front sidewalk, leaning against the "no parking" sign, I think about how grateful I am that Mr. Tutter offered me the job. He seems like such a sweet man. I hope I don't let him down.

A silver Toyota pulls up alongside the curb with the passenger window rolled down. The woman driver leans sideways in her seat to address me.

"Are you the one who called for a ride?"

"I am," I reply, reaching for the rear door handle. "You got here quick."

She doesn't reply, turning her gaze forward as if disinterested in small talk. After I get in, and she pulls away from the curb, the floodgates open like she was waiting to trap me inside before inundating me with her daily drama. I listen and smile, nodding a few times at her stare in the rearview mirror to be polite. Honestly, I couldn't get past the part where she told me she was once almost abducted by aliens when a UFO hovered outside her bedroom window. Everything after that went in one ear and out the other.

Thankfully, we arrive at the garage just as the driver is telling me about her aunt, who has supposedly been struck by lightning four times and can now pick up radio communications from the dead. As far-fetched as her stories were, I suppose they kept my mind distracted enough so as not to stress over the hefty repair bill I was about to pay. I thank the woman and plug in a tip on my phone's app.

I watch the Uber drive off, and then I walk in the front door of Auto Service Center to settle my bill and pick up my car. A different employee, older and broader than Freddie and with much more facial hair, is at the front counter. He greets me with a smile.

"What can I do for you today?" he asks.

"I received a call from Freddie, telling me my car was going to be ready for pickup."

The man shifts his head slightly sideways and looks at me out of the corner of his eyes like he's confused.

"Who did you talk to?" he asks.

"Freddie."

"There's nobody here by that... oh, you mean *Frankie*."

I pull back from the counter a bit and squint. Now *I'm* the one who's confused. I distinctly remember the young man's name being Freddie because of the fond memories of my uncle. I suppose I could have misread his name patch. It's not like I was studying it. But no, even on the phone, he told me it was Freddie. Unless I had it in my head that was his name, so I heard what I wanted to hear. Either way, it doesn't matter.

The burly man continues. "Yeah, he's on his lunch break right now. What's your name?"

"It's Marney Fitzgerald," I tell him.

He punches a few keys on the keyboard and stares inquisitively at the monitor.

"Hmmm.., I don't see you in our system. What were you having done?"

"Freddie.., I mean, Frankie told me the serpentine belt needed replacing."

A few seconds of silence tick by while the man studies the screen. "Nope. No, I don't have anything like that. What's your car?"

"It's a gray Hyundai Elantra," I snap, feeling a little perturbed that they don't have a better system for organizing their jobs.

The large man stares at the computer screen, running his thumb and index finger around his mustache and goatee before turning and looking at some clear plastic pouches hung on a pegboard containing paperwork. He snatches them one at a time and looks in each before returning them to their proper place. Then he turns back to his computer while asking, "Are you sure you dropped your vehicle off *here*?"

"Of course, I'm sure," I answer tersely. "You're the only garage on this road, and I managed to get here just before my car stalled out."

He scratches his head while punching more keys on the keyboard. Then, I think about it and wonder if perhaps I gave him the wrong name.

"What about Leery?" I ask. "Am I in your system as Marney Leery? That's with two Es."

He punches some more keys. I watch his eyes shift from side to side as he reads the screen.

"No, sorry. I don't have anything."

"Oh, come on!" I say with a raised voice. "You have my car."

He grabs a cell phone off the counter and begins to type in some numbers.

"Hold on one sec, ma'am," he says, seeing my frustration. "I'm calling Frankie."

I heard the word *ma'am* like it was a slap. How old do I look? I'm twenty-eight, not *ma'am*. I stand silently at the counter, my blood pressure rising. I shift my gaze to a glass door along the rear wall that gives me a clear view into the garage area. I see the rear panel of a red truck, a black SUV up on a lift, and a silver minivan, but not my car. I turn to look out the front window in case it has already been brought out, thinking maybe I didn't notice it when I exited the Uber, but it's not there.

"Yeah, Frankie, it's Mike." The man's voice snaps my attention back to his conversation. "I got a lady here who says she spoke to you about changing a serpentine belt on her Hyundai. I don't know; hold on a second." He pulls the bottom edge of the phone away from his cheek and looks at me. "When did you say you talked with Frankie?"

"My car died in your parking lot just yesterday. Frankie called me this morning to let me know it was the belt. He said the work would be done before 11:00 and that I could come pick up my car."

"Did you get all that, Frankie?" Mike asks, bringing the lower edge of the phone back to his mouth. "She says you called her this morning." Mike's eyes dart toward me, and his left eyebrow lifts. "Okay. No problem. I'm sorry I bothered you."

He clicks off the phone and brings his hand down to the desk, breathing out with a heavy sigh.

"You must be confused, ma'am," he begins. "Frankie says he didn't call anyone this morning."

He did it again; he called me ma'am. "Oh my God, this is ridiculous," I shout, throwing my hands in the air. "My car is here somewhere. Frankie, or *someone,* took my keys yesterday. That same person called me this morning and told me it was going to be $347 for the work. I'm not making this up. Go look for my Elantra. It's gotta be here."

"Ma'am, it's not in our system, we haven't done any belt changes, and Frankie didn't call you.

I don't know what else to tell you. You must have brought your car to another shop."

I'm getting so angry, my hands begin to shake, and I feel my jaw clenching. These guys are thieves. They took my car and did who knows what with it. They're not going to get away with it. I look at the man with fire in my eyes. "You have my car. I'm calling the police." I pull out my phone as the man crosses his arms and says, "You can call the police all you want; we don't have your car." I flash him a snide look as I turn away from him to speak to the 911 operator.

"Hi. Yes, I'm calling from the Auto Service Center on Meridian Rd. in Longdale. They took my car in for work yesterday, and now they're saying they never had it." I'm so focused on the woman's voice on the other end of the line that I never hear the footsteps behind me until it's too late. But the crack.., that sound is unmistakable. For a second, I think it's thunder, but then the pain blossoms, white-hot. I fall to my knees and try to scream, but my voice comes out as a dry gasp. Light begins to fade as I feel my eyes roll back into my...

Chapter 6

My eyes struggle to open. I feel the pressure of something cold against my cheek, and my head is pounding. When the haze in my eyes has cleared, I see the dank room before me, and it's off kilter. No, it's normal. I'm the one who's sideways, lying on the hard, concrete floor. *What happened? Where am I?*

I set my right palm on the floor by my chest and push myself upright to a seated position. My jaw aches. I bring my hand up to my cheek to massage the pain and feel the dirt and debris fall from my skin at my fingers' touch. Breathing heavily, I glance around the room to catch my bearings. The air smells like rust and damp earth. It looks like I'm in someone's basement. *How did I get here?* I squeeze my eyelids shut and shake my head to clear away the cobwebs. That was a mistake. With every movement of my head, it feels like my brain is crashing against the inside of my skull. I reach up to rub my temple and immediately wince from the pain. My fingers are stained red with blood from grazing over a gash. Something hit me. Some*one* hit me.

My heart begins to race as I quickly scan the room again, searching for any sign of the person who did this to me. There's no movement.

"Hello?" I whisper.

It's quiet except for the sound of my breathing. I lick my dry lips, and my tongue sticks to them like a fly on flypaper. I don't know where I am, but I need to get out of here.

I steady myself and push up from the floor. My legs are wobbly, and my left hip feels a little numb, but I manage to remain on my feet. There's a churning in my stomach, and I feel like I'm going to be sick. I bend over, closing my eyes and propping myself up with my hands against my knees. *Just breathe, Marney. You've got this.*

When the nausea subsides, I push myself upright and exhale through puckered lips. Against the far wall, there is a wooden staircase leading up to what I presume to be the first floor of.., what? Someone's house? A place of business? I have no idea, but it's a way out, and I'm taking it.

With my legs still shaky, I hobble forward as quickly as I can until something snags my ankle and causes me to tumble forward. I land hard on my wrist and feel a sharp pain shoot up my arm. I immediately feel the burning sensation at the base of my palm and watch my wrist swell up like a balloon.

"Shit!" I mutter.

I must have sprained it. *Perfect. Just what I need.* While still lying on the floor, I twist sideways to see what caused me to trip. My eyes widen at the sight.

"Oh fuck! Fuck! What the fuck?"

There's a metal shackle around my ankle with a chain connected to a large eyebolt fastened to the concrete wall. I jolt my body onto my butt and grab for the chain. I yank at it with all my might, feeling my injured wrist howl at me, and my arms weaken. My attention shifts to the shackle as I trace my fingers along the metal clasp, looking for a way to open it. The metal cuts into my ankle as I twist my foot from side to side, trying to loosen the binding. It's no use; I'm only causing myself more damage. My eyes shift to the eyebolt embedded in the wall. Maybe I can unscrew it.

I quickly stand and sprint to the wall, ignoring the biting sting in my ankle. I grasp the bolt with my hands and try to turn it, but my injured wrist makes it nearly impossible to put any strength behind it. It doesn't budge. I look around me for something, *anything*, that I can use to help me. All I see are empty gray surfaces everywhere, with shadows scattered around, taking up residence in the corners of this concrete prison. I try the bolt again. Nothing. An idea comes to me. I lie on my back and place my feet on the wall with the eyebolt between them. I grab the chain near the connection point and pull until it is taut. Then, with my feet firmly planted, I pull with my entire body.

My arms strain, and I feel the muscles in my lower back begin to pull and tear, but I can't give up. My legs begin to quiver, and my jaw is clenched so tightly that I feel I may break some teeth. But still, I can't give up. I extend my head back, resting it on the floor, and pull harder. The veins in my neck pulse as I grunt my desire to be free. Yet still, I can't.., I can't..,

I give up. My arms drop to the hard surface like dead weight. My legs feel like jelly as they slide down to the floor, my calves screaming at me. I look up at the joists in the ceiling, my body exhausted and pushed to its limits. I swallow hard and wonder what I'm going to do. What's my next course of action?

Between my breaths, I hear a faint buzzing sound. I turn my head to my left and feel a bead of sweat run down my forehead to meet the dusty floor. Then I turn my head to the right and notice a glowing light in the shadow in the corner. I spring up onto my elbows to get a better look. It's my phone. Someone is calling me.

I roll onto my knees and scamper toward the vibrating cellphone. Just as I believe salvation is within my grasp, my forward momentum stops, held by the length of the fully extended chain. From this distance, I can see Jason's name scrawled on the phone's lit screen. My heart skips a beat, and my emotions flare. My eyes well up as I sprawl out onto my stomach and stretch my arm out as far as I can. The phone is just out of reach.

"Come on, come on!" I yell, turning back and yanking on the chain once again in desperation. I don't think it moved at all, but I roll back onto my stomach and reach for the phone again, anyway. It's still just out of reach. I pull my shackled leg, feeling the edge of the metal dig deeper into my ankle until I think my foot is going to pop off. It's no use. I can't get there. And then, the call ends, and the screen goes black. Any hope I might have had leaves my body as my shoulders slump to the floor, and my sweaty forehead drops to the concrete.

While I lie there, drained of strength and willpower, languishing in self-pity at my predicament, tears drip from my eyes and crash like boulders to the floor. *Why is this happening to me? Who did this?*

As if in response to my unspoken thought, the door at the top of the staircase creaks open, and light from above permeates the stairs. I jump up onto my feet and back into the hard wall, grabbing the excess chain in my fist as if it provides comfort in my grip, when really, it's the only thing I have that can be used as a weapon.

"Who's there?" I yell, hoping it's someone with a badge who has come to rescue me. I hear the sound of someone stepping onto the first stair tread, and then the door slams shut, enveloping the stairway in darkness once again. "What do you want with me?"

I hear another step taken. Then another, as the person takes their time descending the staircase like they're playing with me.

"What the fuck do you want?" I scream through streaming tears.

I hear the stomping of two more stairs as a figure comes into view. I can't make out who it is with the shadows draped across them.

Then...,

I hear the woman's voice.

"Hello? Hello? You've reached 911; what's your emergency?"

The darkness fades, and my pupils constrict from the sunlight bathing me through the front windows. I'm holding my phone, staring out into a parking lot. The voice clamors again.

"Hello? Are you able to speak? I've dispatched authorities to your location. Can you let me know if you are all right?"

I pull the phone from my ear and look at the screen. I've called 911. I turn and look at the large service center worker behind the counter, his arms crossed in irritation. I speak into the phone.

"I...I..."

I feel lightheaded. Everything becomes topsy-turvy. The room begins to spin. My balance betrays me, and all goes dark.

Chapter 7

The words are soft at first.

"Take it easy, miss."

Then they crash against my skull like a jackhammer.

"Marney! Marney, are you all right?" I recognize the voice as Jason's.

My vision clears to see two people kneeling over me, one of them shining a bright light in my eyes. Behind them, Jason is standing by an open door, looking worried and being held back by a police officer pressing a hand to his chest.

"Easy, sir," the officer says. "Let them do their job."

"Is she all right?" Jason questions, his inquiry directed at the paramedics.

I use my right palm to brush the hand holding the flashlight away and sit up on my elbows. "I'm fine," I state, though I have no idea what is happening. "What's going on?"

One of the two paramedics, a woman, applies pressure to my shoulder to keep me from sitting up further.

"Take it easy, ma'am. You passed out."

"I what? I passed out?"

"That's right," she replies. "It looks like you hit your head, too. That's a nasty bump you've got there." She points to the side of my head.

I reach up and touch the spot where her eyes are focused. I wince and jerk my head away because of how tender it is to the touch. Then, the memory floods back to me like a powerful tsunami crashing into the mainland.

"Wait! No! I was hit with something." I turn my head to the man behind the counter and point. "*He* hit me with something."

The man's eyes bug out of his skull, and he throws his hands up in front of his chest. "Whoa! I didn't touch you, lady."

"You did!" I yell. "You hit me from behind."

"Calm down, now," the officer jumps in. He points to the employee, "I'll start with you. Can you tell me what happened?"

"She came in here looking for her car, which we don't have, and then started accusing us of stealing it or hiding it from her."

"That's right," I speak up heatedly. "I dropped my car off here yesterday, and now they're telling me they don't have it."

Jason jumps in. "Honey, what are you talking about?" he asks.

"I just told you. They're saying they don't have my car, but the guy called me just this morning, telling me I can come pick it up."

"But Marney," Jason swings his arm out the open door into the parking lot, "*I* have your car. Don't you remember? I told you last night I was taking it because my truck was in the shop."

I swivel my head to the side to get a view of the lot. Parked in the first available spot nearest the front door is my little Hyundai.

"Wait. That's not right." I shake my head in confusion. "I broke down yesterday. The car died right in that spot. They said it was the serpentine belt."

"Honey," Jason says softly, stepping in closer and squatting beside me, squeezing my hand. "I've had your car all morning. I drove here from work when they called me. I think the hit to your head has you confused."

"But I..," I stop the words from exiting my mouth when I see the looks on everyone's faces. They think I'm crazy. I'm not crazy. I know what happened. But then, how do I explain the fact that Jason has my car? It doesn't make sense. I know I brought my car here. I'm not making that up.

"Bumps on the head can often cause confusion," the male paramedic states. "You're lucky you don't have a concussion. With a little rest, you should be fine."

"Does she need to go to the hospital?" Jason asks.

"You can't be too careful with head injuries," the woman paramedic responds. "It wouldn't be a bad idea to get that checked out, but that's entirely up to you."

Jason looks at me with sympathetic eyes. "What do you think, hon?"

"I think I'm fine," I answer. "It's like you said, I was just confused for a moment. I remember now. You took the car this morning." *I don't remember that, but we can't afford the ambulance ride, and I'm tired of defending myself when I know what happened.* "I'll be okay once you get me home, and I put my head on a soft pillow."

"Are you sure?" he asks.

I look at him sternly. I know he's only looking out for my well-being, but my stress level is through the roof right now.

"Jason, I'm good. Just help me up." I extend my arms forward, immediately noticing the lack of pain and swelling in my wrist. Jason grabs onto my left, while the male paramedic grabs my right. They gently heave me up, and I let out an audible breath. "Thank you." I look at the paramedics while rubbing my wrist, searching for the pain that should be there but isn't. "I appreciate your help." Then I look at the officer. "I'm sorry you had to come out this way for nothing."

He tips his cap, "It's quite all right, miss."

Finally, I turn to the service center employee. "I'm sorry about the mixup." He puts his hand up in a half-hearted wave, "Yeah."

I turn to Jason and give him an embarrassed grin. "I'm ready to go home now." I take a step, and my leg nearly buckles from the pain. I scream out and reach down with my hand, grabbing my leg below my calf.

"What is it?" Jason questions nervously.

"I don't know," I reply.

"Let's take a look," the female paramedic says, dropping to one knee and rolling up the cuff of my pant leg.

"Wow!" she says.

I peer backwards over my shoulder to get a glimpse of what caused her reaction. I see the large bruise formed around my ankle and the dried blood around a recently-healed open wound.

The woman looks up at me, "Looks like you got your ankle tangled up in something."

Chapter 8

I sit on the couch with my leg raised, two pillows wedged under my ankle. I've been sitting here like a lump, watching Jason cater to me for the past hour like I'm an invalid. That wasn't *my* idea. He wouldn't even let me get up to grab a bottle of water, quickly running to the fridge and delivering it to me like he's my waiter for the evening. He really is a wonderful man. Still, I can't sit here doing nothing, stewing over what had happened. But what exactly *did* happen?

I tried to explain it, but Jason keeps suggesting I must have dreamt it. He doesn't believe me. Why would he? My car is safe, and apparently, has been all day. Why don't I remember Jason telling me about taking it? And why the vivid memory of the car breaking down? Of dropping it off at the garage? Of Freddie helping me and then calling me this morning? And, of course, my ankle.

If I can't get Jason to believe me about the vehicle, how can I tell him about what happened to my ankle? How can I tell him I was shackled and chained in a basement? Whose basement? Where was it? That was real. I know it was. I have the wound to prove it. But then, how did I escape? And how did I get back to the garage?

My God, please don't tell me I'm going crazy. I'm too young to be locked up in a loony bin.

The smell of taco seasoning distracts my troubled thoughts. Maybe I can put this all behind me. Focus on the here and now.

"It smells good, babe," I tell him from my seat on the couch, trying to resemble a calm person.

"I'm trying something new," he tells me. "I added a few different spices to enhance the flavor."

I immediately jump in like it's a competition. "Paprika and Montreal steak seasoning with a tablespoon of honey?" I ask.

He stops stirring the meat and turns to me with a legitimately confused look on his face. "How did you know that?"

I don't have the heart to tell him that he cooked the same thing last week. He doesn't remember. He has an excuse. But then, why is it that I can remember those very details from a week ago, including the specific ingredients he used, but I can't remember about the car or about how I ended up in someone's basement or how I got out of there? So much for putting those thoughts behind me.

"Just a lucky guess," I reply.

"You've got a nose for it; I'll tell you that." He turns back to the stove to continue cooking, probably thinking I have heightened senses.

I roll my ankle slightly to look at the dressing job the paramedics did with the bandage. I felt ridiculous making up the story about how I injured myself.

Oh, I remember now; I caught my ankle under the office chair during my interview. That must have been it. I didn't realize I cut myself.

Sure, they believe *that* stupid story. Oh brother. The paramedic even treated the contusion on the side of my head. The woman believed I had passed out and that the lump was from my fall. Couldn't she tell it was more than that? Was it too impossible to believe someone had hit me from behind? I mean, shit, I'm the one who felt it. Right before I.., before I.., what? Before I woke up, harnessed to a wall in someone's basement one second, and then, sitting on the floor of a service station, being treated by paramedics the next? Okay, when I think of it like that, I understand how it would sound unbelievable. I wouldn't believe me either.

"Are you ready to eat?" Jason announces, stepping from the kitchen with two plates in his hands.

"Yes, please," I reply, swinging my leg off the pillows and setting it softly on the floor. "I'm starving."

Jason places my plate on the coffee table in front of me before sitting down with his plate resting on his lap. We have a little dining room table that seats two just outside the kitchen, but it goes unused except to collect bills and unopened mail. We're both more comfortable eating on the couch in front of the television, anyway.

"I hope you like it," he says, reaching for the television remote and turning up the volume of some show I hadn't been watching. "Oh, before I forget..," he reaches his hand into his front pants pocket, "Phil is picking me up for work in the morning, and then bringing me to pick up my truck at lunch time. You can have your keys back." He pulls the overcrowded keychain from his pocket and tosses it onto the table. It lands with the little pewter cow facing me. I don't think anything of it until I'm finishing up my first taco, and my eyes drift over to notice the creepy bovine staring at me with sorrowful eyes like I'm eating its sibling. But then, before I turn away out of guilt, the text in the word balloon coming from its mouth catches my attention.

Wait! That isn't right, I think. I squeeze my eyes shut tightly and reopen them, thinking I must have read it wrong, but the words don't change. It reads, "You're udder-ly amazing."

I look at Jason in confusion, but he doesn't notice me, his attention fully engrossed on the screen. My head swivels back to the cow, and the words that hadn't been those words before just now. I feel my eyebrows tuck in uncertainty. *What the hell is going on? How hard was I hit?*

Chapter 9

I hear Jason rummaging through the closet. It's enough to disturb my sleep. I let out a hefty sigh and push myself up to a seated position on the bed, pressing my back against the headboard to keep myself propped up.

"Honey, what are you looking for now?" I ask, rubbing my eyes to clear them of the built-up gook in the corners.

"I'm looking for my black shirt with the embroidered emblem on the pocket."

I have to smile and shake my head. "You wore that on Monday."

"No, I didn't," he replies, peeking his head out from the closet door. "It was in here the other day. I remember..," he hesitates, seeing the amused expression on my face. Then, he shifts gears. "We already discussed this, didn't we?"

I flash a sympathetic smile. "We did."

I see his shoulders slump, and his face displays a sudden frown. "I'm sorry," he says in a pathetically sorrowful tone. "I don't know how you deal with me and my Swiss cheese brain."

"Hey," I say sternly. "We talked about this, remember?" Then, I realize my poor choice of words. He probably *doesn't* remember our discussion. I quickly recover. "And if you don't, I'll remind you again, and every time you have any doubt. I don't care that you forget things. I love you. That's not going to change just because you forget which shirt you wore."

"I promise, I'm trying," he responds, as if he feels the need to defend his brain injury.

"Babe, it's fine," I reassure him. "Just pick a different shirt."

He ducks back into the closet, continuing his struggle. I glance at the clock on my nightstand to see it's 6:36. *Why am I awake this early? It's Friday. I don't start my new job until Monday.* I roll my eyes and bring the heel of my palms to my closed eyelids, letting out a yawn. I don't notice it for a few seconds, but everything suddenly becomes silent. Everything except for that damn dripping faucet in the kitchen, which somehow explodes in my ears like I'm right beside it.

Drip. Drip. Drip.

I no longer hear the clothes hangers shifting back and forth along the pole. I peel my hands away from my face and open my eyes. The room is quiet and shaded. The closet door is closed, and Jason isn't in sight.

"Jason?" I call out, leaning forward to get a glimpse into the darkened bathroom. "Babe? Where did you go?" I get no response. *He's a stealthy one this morning. I didn't even hear him leave the room.*

I pull the covers off myself and swing my legs off the side of the mattress, taking care to ease my injured foot to the floor. I stand in a less-than-graceful motion and stretch my arms above my head while yawning a second time. I grab the bunched-up covers I threw off of me and yank them to the edge of the mattress in an attempt to make the bed. I begin to tuck the excess blanket under the pillows when my eyes catch the clock's digital display. In shock, I thrust myself upright.

"What the hell?" I question aloud. The clock now displays a time of 7:41. *That can't be right*, my brain rationalizes. *It was just 6:36 a minute ago. Did I fall back to sleep? No, I couldn't have. But then, I must have. Did I really drift off for an hour? How else can I explain the jump in time? Wow! I must be tired from all the excitement yesterday.*

I shake away the confusion, passing it off as exhaustion. I'm saddened to think that I missed Jason leaving for work. I picture how frustrated he must have become, having a conversation with himself, thinking he was talking with me. Oh well, I'll make it up to him.

Peeling my lips apart, I taste the overnight on my tongue and scrunch my face. My chompers need a brush. I stroll into the bathroom and look at my scraggly hair in the mirror, almost scaring myself. Jason asked how I deal with him, when, after seeing this every morning, I wonder how he deals with me.

I open my mouth and stick out my tongue, spouting the customary "aahhhh," while my fingers weed through my hair to find unruly knots. Between all the freckles, my pale skin shimmers under the sconces on either side of the mirror. I'm a mess. Good thing I don't have anywhere to go today.

I spend the next few minutes brushing my teeth and straightening my hair so it doesn't look like a tumbleweed landed on my head. Then, I hobble toward the living room en route to the kitchen to make myself something for breakfast. As I step out of the bedroom, my peripheral vision catches movement to my right, and I instinctively twist in that direction, sending a sharp pain through my ankle. I have no time to wince as adrenaline kicks in when I spot a young boy sitting in the lounge chair beside the couch.

My eyes explode open, and I recoil, letting out an expletive, "Oh, fu..," before catching myself in the presence of a child. My heart settles, but I stand fixed in the living room, staring at this boy who is staring back at me with no discernible emotion in his expression.

"Hello," I say in a calm but confused voice. "Where did you come from?"

The little blonde-haired boy, barefoot and wearing a black and white striped shirt under denim overalls, doesn't answer, but instead, swings his legs forward and back a few times, clicking his heels against the front of the chair.

Thump.

Thump.

Thump.

Still bewildered, I ask, "What's your name?"

The boy continues his blank stare, kicking the front of the chair harder. I don't know how to handle this. I step forward and ask a third question. "Do you live in this building?"

I don't recall seeing him before. Perhaps his family is new to the building, and he got mixed up with which unit he is in.

Hearing the question, he immediately stops his annoying kicking and shows a modicum of understanding. He raises his right arm and points toward the door.

"Out there?" I question. "You live in one of the other apartments?"

Remaining silent, the boy nods.

"Can you show me?" I ask, encouraging him with hand gestures to draw him toward the exit. He stands and slowly tiptoes to the door, his eyes remaining fixed on mine, like he doesn't trust me enough to even glance away for an instant. *Listen, kid, you showed up in my place. I'm the one with trust issues right now.*

I open the door to escort him to the proper apartment, but he immediately bolts down the hall to the staircase and disappears down them in a flash. I yell, "Hey!" but he doesn't stop. Then the sound of his footsteps fades, and there is silence, as if he were never here. I shake my head, dumbfounded. My eyes shift to the neighbor's door across the hall. Beige. *Wait, wasn't it blue?* I guess they didn't like the new color. I shake my head dismissively. I step back into the apartment and shut the door, wondering why all these weird things keep happening to me. I don't need this right now. I just want things to be normal. Is that too much to ask?

Chapter 10

I gulp down my second cup of coffee without fear of burning my mouth. The coffeemaker burner hasn't worked in almost a year, so the only hot cup is the first-poured cup. I keep meaning to buy a new one, but then reality slaps me in the face; there are more important things to spend our money on. We've lasted this long on lukewarm cups of coffee; we can last a bit longer.

I sit on the edge of the couch, staring at the empty lounge chair, wondering who that little boy was and how he ended up in our apartment. Jason must have forgotten to lock the door when he left. Or maybe he figured it wasn't necessary since I am home every day. I'm just glad it was a harmless boy and not that weirdo from the second floor, Mr. Jeffries. That man gives me the creeps, the way he stares at me whenever he catches me in the hallway or in the parking lot, like he's fantasizing about nasty things. *Get a life, sicko. There are a lot of other women, prettier women, you can be jerking off to.* That thought, alone, makes me want to dry-heave.

My ankle tingles with an itching sensation, and I rotate the back of my foot upward to look at the bandage covering it. The bruising has spread beyond the gauze pad. It's just one more darkened blemish on my pasty-white flesh. At this rate, if I keep getting banged up, I won't need to apply 1000 SPF sunscreen when going out in the sun. The half-hearted attempt to lighten my mood fails miserably. How can I be all rainbows when my brain, along with my skin, keeps going dark? If only I knew what the hell happened to me?

I peel away the tape from my skin and peek under the bandage. The slice in my ankle appears to be doing better, but no amount of healing can soften the memory of how I ended up with it. The basement, the shackle - it was real. My wounded ankle can attest to that. I was trapped somewhere, unable to free myself, and yet, moments later, I wasn't, and I have no explanation of how that could be. Even if what everyone else seems to believe is true, that I fainted and hit my head instead of being struck from behind, my hazy thoughts can't fabricate the injury I sustained. My ankle was most definitely bound. Nobody can explain that or rationalize it away.

A shiver runs down my spine at the thought of what else might have happened to me while I was trapped, unconscious, at the mercy of whoever held me captive. Other than the bump on my head, the cut on my ankle, and the strange bruises on my arm, there doesn't seem to be anything else wrong with me. No welts or swelling. No other cuts or scrapes. No soreness between my legs. I can reasonably assume I wasn't beaten or raped. I don't know; maybe I *am* going crazy.

I get up from the couch and bring my empty cup to the kitchen sink. The previous night's dishes stare at me in disapproval. I'll get to them at some point, but first, a shower. I begin to make my way back to the bedroom when a thought strikes me. I turn and limp to the apartment door, where I lock the deadbolt. I don't need any more unwanted surprises finding their way in.

I step back into the bedroom and gather my things for a comforting shower. Once in the bathroom, I support myself with one hand resting on the vanity while I bend over to remove the bandage from my ankle. I think the water and open air will do it some good. When I stand back up, my eyes immediately catch a glimpse in the mirror of another bruise fashioned on my left arm, opposite the one on the right. I twist my arm upward to look at it.

"What the hell?" I whisper to myself.

The bruise is a lighter shade than the one on my other arm, which might explain why I didn't notice it before now, but the shape has more definition. I sprawl the fingers of my right hand over the four distinct lines on my left bicep. The marks are a perfect match for a hand grip. Not mine, but someone's.

I strain my brain, thinking back to the day before. Jason had helped me to my feet by grabbing hold of my left arm. Could it have been from that? I don't remember him grabbing that hard or causing me discomfort when he pulled me up. Not that I would have noticed, with the aching in my head and the stabbing pain in my ankle. Has my lifestyle over the past few months caused my skin to be so sensitive that I'm susceptible to such bruising from the slightest touch? Shit. I need to renew my membership to the gym and start taking better care of myself. I shake my head and sigh. But first, a steady job with a decent income.

I jump in the shower and scour the walls for a soap message, but find none. Jason must be more upset with me for falling asleep than I thought. Or he's finally given up on the clever messages. Or maybe he forgot. All three are reasonable explanations, and I wouldn't fault him for any of them.

I turn on the water and ease under it to let it wash away the morning's negative thoughts. It will do me good to forget about all the craziness. The car, the basement...it's all behind me. I'll chalk it up to an overactive imagination.

While washing my hair, I think about taking a trip to the grocery store. It would be nice to pick up a few things to have a good meal this weekend. I'm sure Jason won't mind. He's been working so hard these past few months; he deserves it. We *both* do. Besides, with the car not being in the shop, we just saved ourselves $347. Maybe I'll skip the grocery store and make reservations at a nice restaurant instead. Nah. Even with me starting my new job on Monday, we can't start spending money foolishly. We'll have to start saving up for when the baby arrives. That'll be a whole new level of expense. And though I should be concerned, I know it will all be worth it. I feel a smile overtake my face as the thought of raising a little girl outweighs the nervousness and worry.

I rinse away the shampoo and turn the water off, watching a clump of stray hair on the tub floor be carried along to the drain by a stream of water, where it catches on the grate. As I scoop it up to throw it in the trash, it dawns on me that I just thought of having a little girl. Not a child, but a *girl*. Was that me being hopeful, or does something inside my brain already know what I'm having? Does it matter?

That was just the pick-me-up I needed. Between the new job and thoughts of a little girl, I don't think anything can put a damper on my mood. I grab a towel and wipe away the condensation from the mirror to see my bright reflection. Normally, I cringe at the sight, but not today. Today, I find myself staring at a whole new woman peering back at me. She is a strong, positive, beautiful woman, freckles and all, who is going to be a wonderful wife and mother. Things are looking up, and we're going to make the best of it. It's all going to work out. I can feel it.

Chapter 11

Stepping out into the hall, I see Mrs. Blumgard walking in my direction and avert my eyes, hoping she walks by to her apartment. The woman is in her late seventies and can be quite cantankerous when the mood strikes her. I twist the key in the knob to lock the door, and when I turn, the woman is standing before me, her scowled features painfully digging into me like she's about to scold me.

"Oh, hi, Mrs. Blumgard. I didn't see you there. You're looking lovely as usual."

I force a smile to disguise my discomfort. In return, the elderly woman shakes her index finger at me.

"Don't think I don't know what's going on in that apartment of yours," Mrs. Blumgard replies. "I have half a mind to call the landlord on you."

"Excuse me?" I answer, both confused and upset for being verbally accosted by this woman.

"Don't pretend you don't know what I'm talking about," she continues. "The loud ruckus in the middle of the night. The screaming."

The *screaming?*

"You're lucky the police didn't show up," she continues.

"Mrs. Blumgard, I don't know what you're talking about. Whatever you heard, it wasn't coming from our apartment."

"Are you calling me a liar?"

"I'm not saying that at all," I reply as politely as possible. I don't let it show how upset I am that I even have to defend myself over this absurd accusation. I can't afford for Mrs. Blumgard to give the landlord a reason to kick us out. "I'm sure you heard *something*, Mrs. Blumgard; I'm simply letting you know that it wasn't us."

"I'm keeping a sharp eye on you," she screeches, like fingernails on a chalkboard. "Both you and that Toby are nothing but trouble."

She storms past me to her apartment door before I can correct her. I continue to stare in her direction, flummoxed, until she disappears into her unit.

"Toby?" I whisper to myself, half-smirking. I can't believe she forgot Jason's name. He and I have had multiple conversations with Mrs. Blumgard, and she never once forgot. And what's that about screaming? Is she going completely batty? If someone were screaming in the middle of the night, Jason and I would have heard it. And then it would have kept me from sleeping for the rest of the night. I think the woman is starting to show her age. Or she's going completely insane.

I shake it off and take a final glance at the neighbor's beige door before ambling down the hall to the staircase. At least my ankle is holding out. That's a plus. With no elevator in this dump, the stairs are already a difficult challenge to navigate, let alone for a pregnant cripple such as myself. Fun times. Maybe it wouldn't be too awful if we *were* to get evicted. There's gotta be better places out there than this.

Stop thinking that way, Marney. It isn't that bad. And the rent is...almost manageable.

I make my way down to the first floor, thankfully avoiding Mr. Jeffries' unnerving stare. I step out into the back lot and head straight for the rear corner. It had rained overnight, leaving puddles that reflect the gray sky like tiny mirrors. I walk between the cars, my shoes making sucking sounds on the wet pavement with every step.

When I have a clear view of the dumpster, I feel my chest tighten. The car isn't where Jason had parked it when he drove us home. I turn in place, scanning the row of vehicles behind me. I pivot to the left on my good heel and finally see it – four spaces over in the second row, half-crooked, nose pointed toward the street. That's not where it was parked. I *know* it's not.

I unlock the door and hop in. I immediately notice how far back the seat is, like someone much taller than either of us had been inside. What the hell is going on? While I finagle with the lever under the seat to pull it forward, my eyes catch movement in the rearview mirror of someone in the backseat. *Who is that?* I snap my head around to look, but there's nobody there. I lean over the center console between the front seats to get a better look at the floor on both sides to make sure they didn't duck out of sight. Nobody.

You're really letting your thoughts get to you, Marney. It's all in your head.

With my heart pounding, I turn back and see a figure standing in front of my car. I let out a startled scream before I realize it's Mr. Jeffries, staring at me with his crooked smile. He flashes me a wave as his tongue flicks out to wet his lower lip, then he casually trods off toward the rear entrance of the building. I try to catch my breath while I watch him disappear through the doorway. I close my eyes, drop my chin to my chest, and rub the tension from my forehead, exhaling slowly. When I reopen my eyes, I glance again in the rearview mirror out of caution. There's nothing but an empty backseat and a row of cars behind me. I let myself calm down for a few seconds before tugging at the lever between my legs to reposition the seat. My eyes dart left and right across the parking lot, looking for any other potential signs of life that could suddenly jump out at me. When I'm satisfied there's nobody else around to give me a heart attack, I start the car and drive out of the parking lot.

I stop at the little market in the center of town. It's very charming with a small-town feel. I don't recognize most of the brands, but the products never let me down. Their selection is decent enough for our needs. Mr. Mansfield, the owner, is always quite pleasant and will occasionally offer me discounts, knowing about our financial struggles. I've told him on numerous occasions that he doesn't have to do that, but he's insistent. He's a sweet man. You don't find that kind of customer care at the chain stores.

I can't wait to tell Mr. Mansfield the news of my new job. I'm sure he'll be ecstatic for me, and I will feel better for him to know we won't need his charity. I know he doesn't think of it like that, but that is what it is. He does so much to help his customers. I'll be more than happy to pay full price, and maybe a little extra when I can, to pay him back for all he's done.

I step into the small grocery store and am greeted by Mr. Mansfield's warm smile and customary greeting.

"Welcome to Mansfield's Market," he belts out before realizing it's me. "Ah, Marney. How are you this fine Friday? We're having a sale on peaches this week, and pork sausages are forty percent off."

He's a lovely man, always cheerful, never crotchety like some other folks I know. *I'm looking at you, Mrs. Blumgard.* Though in his late sixties, his exuberance is that of a young man, as is his full head of jet-black hair, except for some graying over the temples. He has a certain twinkle in his eye, and his mustache curls up onto his rounded, rosy cheeks from his constant smile.

"Hello, Mr. Mansfield," I respond with a smile of my own. "I'm doing well, thank you. I actually have some exciting news to share."

His face lights up, and he reaches forward like a fatherly figure and gently places his hands on my upper arms.

"That's wonderful, my dear," he says. "I love hearing good news. What is it?"

"Well," I begin, "as of this coming Monday..."

I don't get the chance to finish my sentence, as a loud crashing noise from aisle three, like a jar of spaghetti sauce smashing to the ground, interrupts my thoughts. Mr. Mansfield releases me and drops his arms to his side as he turns his head over his shoulder to look behind him. When he turns back to me, his expression has shifted to something I have never seen from him before. His eyes are narrow, cold. His nose is wrinkled, his lips pursed, and his chin is quivering like he's struggling to keep from exploding into a seething tirade of expletives.

"Excuse me," he says through curled lips and gritted teeth. "There's something I must deal with."

I watch him storm off, swerving around the large bin of produce near the front of the store, before ducking out of sight into one of the aisles. Seconds later, I hear Mr. Mansfield's voice erupt into such rage, castigating one of his employees over the mishap. I'm frozen in shock by the front door, unable to move until I hear several more jars crash to the floor, no doubt the employee's response to Mr. Mansfield's handling of the situation. I slowly shuffle backwards out of the front door, imagining the employee's next course of action being removing his smock and throwing it in his employer's face.

As I stampede through the parking lot back to my car, I'm shook at the thought of Mr. Mansfield's unexpected reaction, the sudden change in his demeanor. He's always been such a delightful man. To hear him scream the way he did, to humiliate his employee like that, is something I never imagined could come from his mouth. Maybe he's not the man I thought he was. I wonder if other customers have seen that side of him before. My heart weeps at the thought, and I'm suddenly no longer interested in grocery shopping. We have enough ramen noodles and boxes of macaroni and cheese to get by for a few more days. We might even have some snack cups of Jell-O for dessert. It's not exactly what I'd hoped to surprise Jason with this weekend, but there's always next week to look forward to.

Yeah, I think, looking at my pale reflection in the rearview mirror and forcing a smile, *next week will be different.*

Chapter 12

I arrive back at the apartment building some-what flustered. I intentionally park in the first spot to the left of the building's rear entrance, so I know exactly where I am. I shift my eyes to the tenement's rear glass door to make sure Mr. Jeffries isn't lurking inside. I've had enough of people's unusual behavior for one day; I don't think I could handle any perverted ogling from my downstairs neighbor.

I step out of the vehicle and walk to the front of the car with my phone in hand. I snap a picture of my exceptional parking job to retain as evidence. I'll know for sure if someone is playing a game with me. I scan the parking lot a final time before turning and heading inside.

The throbbing in my ankle returns as I strain myself going up the two flights of stairs. I thought the aching was behind me, but apparently, going up that many stairs is a bit too strenuous. I shuffle to our apartment, my ankle screaming with each step, and when I unlock the door and swing it open, there is an envelope on the floor waiting for me.

Not another threat of eviction. I can't handle that today.

I bend over and pick it up, flipping it over to see if there is anything written on it. There isn't. I step into the apartment, and as I turn to close the door, I pause, noticing the neighbor's door across from ours is now a vibrant red. I feel myself cringe at the color before closing the door the rest of the way. *Beige, blue, red.., can't those people decide what they like? I wasn't even gone that long. How did they paint it so quickly?*

Once I'm inside the calm of my own apartment, the infernal dripping of the kitchen faucet catches my attention, as each drop explodes in my ears like landmines going off.

Drip. Drip. Drip.

I can't deal with that right now. My ankle is throbbing and needs attention first. I place the envelope on the dining room table and limp my way to the bathroom. From the second drawer of the vanity cabinet, I pull out a bottle of Tylenol and pop two tablets in my mouth to quell the pain. I could probably manage without, but between the annoyance of the dripping faucet and the arrival of probably yet another eviction letter under our door, it will do me some good by taking the edge off.

I toss the bottle back in the drawer and lean my weight on the vanity counter, staring at myself in the mirror. I step back to catch a full view of myself and scrunch my nose at what I see. I lift the lower hem of my shirt to expose my abdomen, which doesn't make me feel any better. It's definitely seen fitter days. I bring my hand up to gently rub my stomach before turning sideways to get a look at my profile. It's too early for a baby bump, but I force my stomach outward to get a glimpse of the future. Am I ready for the discomfort of sitting and sleeping? The back pain? Am I ready for the odd cravings, the weight gain, and later, the stretch marks?

Am I ready to be a mom?

I relax and let my stomach spring back to its normal position, suddenly feeling even more self-conscious about my figure. I feel my shoulders drop, then my chin, before letting out a defeated sigh.

I tiptoe out of the bathroom to keep the skin on my ankle from stretching and yelling at me. When I get back to the living room, I grab the unopened envelope from the table and plop myself down on the couch with my injured leg propped up on a pillow. I'm about to open the letter when I feel my pocket vibrating. I pull my phone out and am surprised to see it's the auto shop calling me. I hit the speaker button.

"Hello?"

"Hi, is this Marney Fitzgerald?"

"It is."

"This is Freddie from Auto Service Center. I'm calling to remind you we still have your car. It's ready for pick up."

"My car?" I question. "My car's not in the shop. I just parked it. And that's very funny, 'Freddie,' or 'Frankie,' or whoever you are."

"Um, ma'am, I'm talking about the gray Hyundai Elantra. You broke down in our parking lot the other day. We spoke on the phone yesterday."

"Yeah, I know what my car is," I answer snidely. "And it's Miss, damn it, not ma'am. Listen, I don't know what kind of game you're playing, but we've already gone through this. I just got out of my car a few minutes ago. Nice try, though."

"I'm confused," the man on the other end states. *"Is this Marney Fitzgerald, owner of a gray Hyundai Elantra, license plate number 669 PZL?"*

"Yes, and you're obviously a prank caller who has done your homework. Now, I'd appreciate it if you stopped calling me. How did you get my number, anyway?"

"You gave it to me when you handed me the keys, and we did the paperwork," he replies heatedly. *"I'm looking at your car right now. They just brought it out and parked it out front."*

"Oh, really?" I question, swiping at my phone's screen to open up my photos. "How can *you* be looking at my car when *I'm* looking at..,"

I freeze, mid-sentence, as the blood drains from my face. I hear each bothersome, liquid explosion from the kitchen sink.

Drip. Drip. Drip.

I'm staring at a picture of a vehicle, but it's not mine. I swipe my thumb to the right. Nope. I swipe twice to the left. Nope. Back once to the right to land on the same picture. Why am I staring at a black Acura?

"Miss? Are you there?"

"Y-yes, I'm here. I just.., I need to think for a moment."

"I don't know what to tell you," the man says. *"Perhaps you're confused. I promise you, it's parked right outside our window. We changed the serpentine belt for you. Now, I don't mean to cause any trouble, but we can only keep it here for a couple of days before we start charging a daily storage fee. We're open until six tonight, and then, nine 'til two tomorrow. I have to get back to work, but I hope you have a wonderful evening."*

"Wait, wait," I yell at the phone while I frantically pat myself down, searching for the keys. "You said I handed you my keys?"

"That's right."

"Can you tell me what the keychain is?"

If this *is* some kind of prank, if I didn't drop my car off at the garage, there's no way he'd know what my keychain is.

"Hold on a second," he says. I hear him put the phone down, and with a muffled voice, he asks someone named Hank for the keys. A few seconds later, he picks up the receiver and answers, *"Yeah, I gotta cow here."*

My first thought is, *Lucky guess?* Then he continues.

"It's got the words 'Have you heifer been in love' coming out of its mouth in one of those word balloons."

I stare silently at the screen, my mouth agape. My thoughts are all over the place, but I can't seem to pull them together coherently to say anything.

"Hello? Hello, Miss? Are you there?"

I try to speak, but nothing comes out. Then I hear the line click, and the call ends.

Chapter 13

I'm staring out the back door of the apartment building into the parking lot, but I still can't believe what I'm seeing. Parked in the first spot to the left of the rear entrance is a vehicle that is not mine. But that can't be right. I know I parked there less than twenty minutes ago. I took a picture and reviewed it right after. It was my Hyundai. But now, like so many other things lately, even that has betrayed me and changed to this other vehicle in front of me. What the hell is going on?

I feel myself getting woozy and shuffle backward to sit on the staircase. Am I going crazy? I prop my elbows on my bent knees and rest my forehead in my palms, taking deep breaths. Something isn't right. I feel nauseous. Shit!

I get up and quickly hobble up the stairs to the third floor, pushing past the ache in my ankle. I quicken my pace more on the straightaway down the hall from the top of the staircase to my apartment door, where I barge through without bothering to close it behind me. My only thought is getting to the bathroom on time. I ignore the pain from every step until I crumble beside the toilet, offering up a sacrifice to the porcelain god. When I think I've discharged every bit of my stomach, and I fall back on my butt in relief, the feeling comes upon me again like an active geyser ready to explode. I lunge my upper body forward and expel the remainder of whatever's left in me into the bowl.

My eyes remain closed as I reach up and pull the handle to flush. For a moment, I feel so weakened that I can't keep my head upright, and I let my cheek fall softly onto the back of my hand, which is on the front rim of the cold porcelain. It takes a few seconds before it dawns on me that my face and lips are dangerously close to a place never meant for them. My eyes shoot open, and I force my head up, pushing myself away from the bowl and back to my feet. I wipe the beads of sweat from my forehead and shake my head in frustration. It's only my first bout, and I can already tell I'm going to hate morning sickness.

I grab the towel hanging from the wall mount and wipe my lips. I lean forward over the sink and turn the cold water on, letting my forearms rest on the counter while I wag my index finger under the stream until I feel it's cold enough. Letting a decent amount pool in my palm, I sip it in and swish it around my mouth to remove any unwanted remnants before spitting it out. After a splash over my face and another round of brushing, I'm feeling much better.

I walk through the bedroom, glancing at the unmade bed, and decide it can wait. When I get to the doorway, I freeze in my tracks and feel my muscles grow rigid before letting out a breath.

Across the living room, standing in the open front door, is the little blonde boy who'd been in the apartment earlier this morning. He was motionless, staring at me again with those expressionless eyes.

"Oh, hi," I say, after gathering myself and trying to act pleasant. "You're back."

I walk out into the living room, heading toward the boy cautiously so as not to scare him.

"You're not going to run off again, are you?" I ask.

He doesn't answer, but he doesn't budge either, which, I guess, *is* an answer. I grab the doorknob and stare down at him with as friendly a smile as I can muster.

"Are you lost?" I ask.

He shakes his head no.

"Are your parents home?"

Again, he offers a head shake.

"Oh, well, do you know where they are?"

He nods.

I raise my eyes to glance down the hallway. There's no stirring or anyone about.

"You're not a very talkative one, are you?" I question playfully.

He continues to stare blankly at me like he's waiting for an invitation to come inside. *It didn't stop you the first time.*

"My name is Marney. Would you like to come in?"

His eyes drop from mine and shift forward into the apartment, darting left to right as if he is assessing the level of danger if he should accept. Then, he charges past me and resumes his spot in the lounge chair.

"Sure, make yourself at home," I mumble quietly under my breath. Just as I go to swing the door shut, I catch sight of the neighbor's door and do a double-take. It's beige again. I can't keep up with the Joneses. Or "Larson"s, as the nameplate states. I roll my eyes and close the door.

I turn to face the boy, who is now back to thumping his heels against the legs of the chair.

Thump. Thump. Thump.

Drip. Drip. Drip.

Thump. Thump. Thump.

I squeeze my eyes closed, rub my right temple vigorously to dispel the annoyance from my mind, and then open them to see the boy's vacant stare still trained on me.

"So, which floor do you live on?" I ask, as I slowly pace forward and slide onto the couch to the boy's right. He doesn't respond, only continues to kick the chair with the back of his bare heels.

Thump. Thump. Thump.

"Do you have a name?"

And just like that, the boy's kicking stops as he leans forward in his chair and whispers, "It's me, Toby."

He says it in a way as if I'm supposed to know who he is, but instead, my thoughts shift to Mrs. Blumgard's earlier comments. She mentioned a Toby. She also mentioned he was "nothing but trouble." Could this be who she was talking about? I mean, I get it. He shows up out of the blue and walks into people's apartments uninvited, staring at you through creepy little eyes. But he's just a kid. Other than being a little odd and maybe a bit too quiet, which, let's face it, is not the worst a kid could be, he doesn't seem that bad.

"Well, it's nice to meet you, Toby," I offer, extending my arm to him. He looks at it cautiously and stays put. "Right," I say, pulling my hand back to my side.

I think my facial expression must have looked as though I was disappointed, because from my reaction, he stands up, slowly tiptoes closer to me, and extends his hand to shake. I smile and gently accept. When we release, he doesn't go back to his seat, but instead, continues to stand in front of me. It makes me feel a bit uncomfortable, so I quickly shift to hostess mode.

"Would you like something to drink?" I ask, standing and stepping toward the kitchen. "I think we might have some juice. Or maybe a Jell-O?"

And then, he says something that, for some reason, stops me from continuing.

"We?"

I draw my eyebrows in and turn to face the boy, thinking it a strange question to ask.

"That's right," I answer. "I live here with my husb.., I mean, my boyfriend, Jason. He's at work right now."

With a deadpan face, the boy says, "No, he's not."

I tilt my head slightly, confused at the boy's comment.

"Yes, he is," I say, trying to be polite, but annoyed that the boy would say such a thing. "Why would you think he's not? Have you met Jason? Where do you think he is?"

I can tell from the boy's wide-eyed stare that my barrage of questioning scares him.

"I shouldn't have come here," he responds, side-stepping to the door.

"What?" I reply, unsure of what is happening. "Wait!" I yell to Toby as he opens the door. "I'm sorry if I scared you."

"I have to go."

"You don't have to go if you don't want to."

He steps out into the hall and turns to face me, reaching into the pocket of his denim overalls.

"I only came to return these to you," he says, pulling his hand from his pocket. "You dropped them in the stairwell as you ran by me."

He hands me a set of keys. I immediately notice the cow with its word balloon. These are my car keys. The garage *doesn't* have them, after all. I'm *not* going crazy. It must have been the nausea, the morning sickness. It was playing tricks with my head.

"Thank you," I say, still staring down at my keys. "I didn't even see you when I..." My words trail off when I look up and see that Toby is gone. He must have run off again. *He's a quick one,* I think.

I feel bad that I scared the boy away, but I'm thankful he was kind enough to deliver my keys back to me. I should know better than to believe anything Mrs. Blumgard says. *"Nothing but trouble."* Ha! He's a nice boy.

I shake my head and slowly disappear back inside the apartment, paying little attention to the neighbor's now green door.

Chapter 14

vening rolls in faster than expected, the sun's light quickly fading behind the distant horizon of colorless trees and dilapidated apartment buildings. Jason will be home soon, and I breathe a sigh of relief.

I stare out the living room window overlooking the parking lot, where my Hyundai has mysteriously returned to its rightful spot, under the flickering light of a nearby lamppost. I can't believe how much the pregnancy is already affecting me. I've heard horror stories of how raging hormones can play havoc with a woman's body and mind, but I didn't think it would be this bad, or so soon. I should probably pick up one of those motherhood books. *Perhaps one titled, "The Horrors of Pregnancy."* I laugh to myself.

I back away from the window just enough that the outside lamp light fades from sight, turning the

81

glass into a black mirror. My reflection looks strange, blurred at the edges, like I'm half-here and half-somewhere else. Behind me, for just a second, I think I see someone standing – tall, older, motionless, wearing a maintenance uniform. I turn, but there's nobody there. More hormones.

Then, a knock at the door startles me. I slide my hands up and down my arms to dispel the goosebumps as I make my way to the door. When I open it, an older gentleman is standing in the hall, holding a clipboard. I immediately catch myself flashing a stunned look as he is wearing a maintenance uniform similar to the one I thought I saw in the reflection.

"M-may I help you?" I manage to stutter out.

"Mrs. Leery?"

"Fitzgerald," I correct him. "I'm not married."

He squints at his sheet. "It says here your place is due for an inspection."

"What? Nobody told me about that."

"It's just routine, ma'am. But I can come back another time if it's more convenient."

Again with the *'ma'am'*? At least coming from an older man, it doesn't seem as jagged.

"No, no," I relent. "It's fine. You can…,"

He steps inside before I even finish my sentence, as if he had no intention of coming another day.

"It's good that you're here, actually," I tell him, as he waddles his way to the front window. "The kitchen faucet has been…"

"You've got a little mold here," he interrupts, rubbing a gloved index finger along the sill.

"Mold?" I question.

"Yup. A little bit. I'll make a note of it and see if I can get that taken care of before it gets worse. It's not healthy to be breathing that in, especially in your condition."

I step back, shocked at his comment. "In my condition?"

He swings his body around and points at my midsection.

"Oh, I'm sorry," he says, looking slightly flustered. "I thought you were pregnant."

I instinctively bring my hand to my stomach, though there is nothing to feel yet, nothing showing, nothing to prove I am anything but a normal, ghost-faced, Irish woman.

"I-I am," I state confusedly. "How did you..?"

"I knew it," he interjected excitedly. "I could tell when I first saw you. You have that glow around you."

That's just the brilliant light reflecting off my pale skin, sir.

"My wife was the same way. There was a special aura around her, too. It's a beautiful thing."

I pull my eyebrows in. "Thank you?" I say it as more of a question, unconvinced.

"Do you have a name picked out for her yet?" he asks.

My jaw hangs open, stunned. How does he know it's a girl? Seeing my reaction, the man flops his hand over to dismiss his comment.

"I'm sorry, ma'am. I won't bother you with any more of my nonsense." He swiftly walks past me into the bedroom. "I'll get on with it. Bathroom this way?" It's a question, but he confidently strides forward like he's done it a hundred times. I guess he has, since the apartments are all the same in this building. I follow him in, glancing at the still unmade bed, and feel a twinge of embarrassment.

In the bathroom, he squats beside the toilet and reaches around to the backside, feeling the knob for leaks. *Sure, check the non-problematic water-thingy.* Meanwhile, the drips from the kitchen sink continue to echo behind me like a drum solo. The same slow, hollow drip.

Drip. Drip. Drip.

"Do you think you can do something about the kitchen faucet?" I ask.

"The kitchen faucet?"

"Yeah. It won't stop dripping. Day and night, it's a constant annoyance."

"I can check it out," he says, standing and squeezing his clipboard to his side.

"Thank you," I tell him, leading him back toward the living room. "It's so loud. I can't believe you didn't say anything when you first came in."

I walk him to the edge of the kitchen, but when we get there, the faucet is no longer dripping, and the sink is dry.

"I swear, it was dripping just a moment ago," I say, desperate for him to believe me.

He flashes me a skeptical glare, but quickly covers it up.

"This sorta thing happens all the time," he says. "It's probably a loose valve."

He bends over and opens the bottom cabinets to expose the plumbing. After only a few seconds of inspection, his voice echoes out from underneath.

"Uh-huh. There's your problem." He maneuvers his head out from inside the cabinets and stands beside me, pointing. "See that little black, plastic plug sticking out of the pipe?"

I bend over and lean in to get a closer look at what he's talking about. I don't remember seeing anything sticking out...

The smell catches my attention first, like antiseptic. Only, it isn't. And then, it's too late. The damp cloth smothers my nose and mouth, and I inhale the sweet, minty, yet pungent odor. My vision begins to blur almost immediately. The man yanks at my hair, pulling my head back. I reach for his hand, but he's too strong. A second later, my face rushes toward the front of the sink with force, and my forehead smashes against the edge of the countertop. I fall backward on my butt while liquid stings my left eye. Everything spins around me until the kitchen slants sideways, and everything goes black.

Chapter 15

My eyes flutter open. I'm woozy. Dizzy. The lights are fading in and out like they're alive. Breathing. Sound is muffled. My mouth is dry. I lick my lips and taste granular dust particles. My head hurts. I try to bring my hand to my head, but it doesn't respond to my thoughts. I try my other arm, and I feel the ache in my shoulder scream at me, but still, it doesn't budge. That's when I remember, and my eyes shoot open wide. Panicked, my breathing becomes rapid and shallow.

The basement! No. I'm somewhere else. I'm in a brighter room, lying sideways on a couch, my head compressed into a cushion. I try to lift myself, but feel the pressure of something across my forehead holding my head down. Again, I try to summon my arms, but it's no use. I feel the rope, burning into my wrists behind my back. I'm tied down. I command my bent legs to kick, but as they try, I feel my arms get yanked downward, nearly pulling my shoulders out of their sockets. I'm not just tied-I'm *hog*-tied.

My eyes dart in a zig-zag motion, scanning all I can see in my limited view. Where the hell am I? It looks like someone's living room. The wall in front of me is covered in a light green wallpaper, with some of the seams peeling away. Food and drink stains paint a lurid picture on the tan carpeting covering the floors. There's a small, wheeled TV stand against the wall in front of me, an old, dusty tube television sitting on it, bowing the top shelf from its weight. What is this place? How did I get here? I squeeze my eyes shut and think.

Think, damn it!

Wait. I was in my apartment. Someone knocked on the door. An inspector? No, a maintenance man. He called me Mrs. Leery. That's Jason's last name, not mine. He grabbed me. He did something to me.

The smell of antiseptic permeates my nostrils, and my eyes snap back open.

He drugged me! He knocked me out with something. And then, the vivid memory of my head meeting the counter makes my forehead begin to sting. I want to scream, but think better of it. I don't know if the person who did this to me is nearby. I don't want to alert them that I'm awake. I begin to tremble, and my eyes tear up. What the fuck is going on here? Who was that guy? He wasn't a maintenance man. Why has he done this? What does he want with me? I tug my arms again, but the straining only weakens me further. I try to twist my head, but feel the strap or whatever it is scrape across the open gash in my forehead. I bite my lip, holding back a scream.

Then, I hear a noise behind me. It's something rattling, metal on metal. It's the sound of a key in a doorknob. Someone's coming. My heart pounds so hard in my chest, I think it's going to erupt from my sternum like in an alien movie. What do I do? What do I do? There's nothing *to* do. I'm helpless, immobile.

I hear voices ring out as the door swings open. I close my eyes, pretending to be unconscious. I feel a cold draft rush over me as the chill from the outside storms in and sweeps across my skin.

"Don't give me that shit. You know as well as I do, the refs blew the call."

"They didn't blow the call. Rice clearly had one foot out of bounds."

It's two men's voices. They're getting louder. Closer.

"Only *after* the completion, and after he'd already taken two steps."

"Whatever. How much did you lose?"

"Two grand."

"Fuck, man. You're in a rut."

"No shit. How's she looking?"

"She's still out."

"Is she still dry?"

"No piss."

I can feel them. They're right in front of me. I can feel their eyes on me, looking me up and down, ideas swirling in their heads. I remain still, calm. *Don't let them see you shaking.*

"What's on now?" one of them asks.

"The remote's on the stand," the other replies, his voice farther away now.

I hear a refrigerator door open, glass bottles clinking together. The television explodes in my ears, almost causing me to react, but I hold steady.

"Here," the returning man says. "What'd you find?"

"It's the Tyson/Long fight."

"That's right! Fuck! It's Wednesday already."

I listen as the two men provide commentary on the boxing match. *Did he say Wednesday?* I slowly ease my left eye open, hoping they're too engrossed in the television to care to glance back. They are standing two feet from me, facing away, so I can't get a look at their faces. One is large, heavy-set, with his pants falling halfway down his ass. The other is leaner, more fit, his short-sleeved shirt exposing his muscular arms.

And then, something strikes me. A familiarity. His shirt. There's a logo on it. It looks like.., like..,

"Marney."

I feel his hands upon me, and I jump up to a seated position, letting out a yell.

"Let go of me!"

Jason recoils, his appearance distressed.

"Whoa! It's me. You're okay. You were asleep."

"Jason?"

I quickly swivel myself on the couch to look around me and determine I'm in my living room.

"Yeah. Are you good now? That must have been some dream."

"Dream?" I squint my eyes and wrinkle my nose. *But it was so real.* I still feel jumpy and glance behind me as if someone might be there, ready to grab me.

"Anyway," Jason says, "I just wanted to let you know I'm heading out. There's something I've gotta take care of. I won't be out too long."

"Out too long?" I question. "Didn't you just get home from work?"

"Home from work?" he repeats with an odd look as he leans in to kiss my forehead. "That nap did a number on you. When was the last time I had to work on a Sunday?"

His words hit me hard. I open my mouth to say something as he walks to the door, but I can't quite gather my thoughts enough to articulate them into words. Did he say Sunday? But how..?

When the door shuts behind him, I look to the window, where sunlight is pouring in through the crack in the curtain. It shouldn't be this bright. It was just nighttime. I get up from the couch and walk over, noticing my ankle doesn't hurt as much. When I pull the curtains open, the sunlight blinds me for a moment, and I throw my hand up in front of my eyes. Fighting off little black spots in my vision, I scan the parking lot below. I see my car parked by the dumpster *(didn't I park next to the rear entrance?)*, but I don't see Jason's truck anywhere. He couldn't have driven off already; he just walked out the door.

Right, Marney. Just like it can't be daytime or Sunday right now.

Wait! Sunday? How the hell is it Sunday? What happened to Saturday? How could I have missed an entire day? I am freaking losing it!

I feel a headache coming on, and close my eyes to shield them from the bright sun. I take in a deep breath and blow it out slowly, calming my nerves. When I reopen them, I'm back to sitting on the couch, and the room is darker. I look toward the window; the curtains are closed with no light shining through them. I shake my head, trying to loosen the cobwebs. Was it day or night? I reach up and pinch the bridge of my nose between my thumb and finger. And then I hear it.

Drip. Drip. Drip.

I let out a sigh and, frustratingly, turn my head toward the kitchen. As they pass by the dinette table, my eyes catch the envelope I'd placed on it, but the envelope's flap is now open. I don't remember opening it. Did Jason?

Curious, I get up to retrieve the piece of mail and immediately notice the pain in my ankle has returned. Or had it ever gone? I don't know anymore. Everything is off kilter.

I grab the envelope from the table and pull the folded letter out. My eyes widen at the seven words scribbled on the paper.

Did you think we wouldn't find you?

What the hell is this? What does it mean? Find who? Does Jason know about this?

Of course, he does, Marney. He's the one who opened the letter.

Was this meant for him? For me? Was it shoved under the wrong door?

I feel my hands begin to quiver. I fold the letter and work diligently to work it back into the envelope, but my shaky hands won't cooperate. Then, I stop the struggle when my eyes glimpse something that shouldn't be, can't be, and it catches me off guard. I drop the stationery to the floor, rolling my palms upward. My mind races as I stare at the darkened rope burns around my wrists.

Chapter 16

The second hand on the clock ticks a rhythmic beat while I stare at my half-empty cup of tea beside the empty plastic container of Jell-O. It was all I could manage to eat. Between the nausea of morning sickness and this overwhelming feeling of anxiety, I can't keep anything down.

Without shifting my head, my eyes drift to the envelope on the table. I'd read the letter over and over before tucking it back in its holder.

Did you think we wouldn't find you?

What does it mean? Who is it from? Was it even meant for us? It must be a mistake.

Jason's words rush back to me.

There's something I've gotta take care of.

He didn't elaborate. What did he need to do? Where was he going? I can't help but think the worst. I know he opened the letter and read it, but he didn't say anything to me about it before he left. I was so groggy and confused when I woke, I didn't think to question him. And then, the whole deal with finding out it's Sunday already..,

What the hell? I missed an entire day. How?

My eyes shift back to my lap, where my arms lie like dead weight across my thighs. I pull my right sleeve up to expose my wrist and trace my left index finger across the tender wound, a scarred bracelet of red flesh burned into my skin by a rope that had bound me. How? Wasn't it only a dream? I remember snippets. A couch, a television, my arms and legs tied. And voices. There were two men. Wasn't there something about one of them? I can't remember. It all fades as quickly as it comes to me. But the burns on my wrists haven't faded. They tell me a different story-that it couldn't have been a dream. I was there, in that room, on that couch. But then I wasn't. I was here on my own couch. And an entire day has vanished.

What is wrong with me? Am I cracking up? One minute, I'm in some basement somewhere, shackled to the wall, then I'm not. Next, I'm in someone's living room, tied up on a couch, only to wake up safe in my own apartment. Is my mind playing some kind of masochistic game? I know what happened. I was shackled. I was tied. I can't just explain it away like it was only a dream. My injured ankle and wrists would strongly argue. Fuck!

I gently rub my opposite wrist before reaching for my phone. Jason hasn't responded to my texts, and my last five attempts to call him have all gone unanswered. Will the sixth time be the charm? It bothers me that his inbox is full; I can't even leave him a voicemail. I've told him at least a dozen times he needs to clean that up, but with his horrible memory, it continues to go unresolved. That's it; no more excuses. When he gets home, I'm doing it for him.

I listen as the line rings. Twice. Three times. Four.

Come on, Jason, answer your damn phone!

After the fifth ring, it bounces to the all-too-familiar recording, telling me the person I'm trying to reach is unavailable, and that their inbox is full. Then the call abruptly ends. *Shit!*

I'm getting antsy. My leg begins to bounce up and down, and nothing I do or think about seems to help. Confusion gives way to anger.

Where the hell are you, Jason? Answer your fucking phone!

Anger gives way to worry.

Please come home. Call me back to tell me you're safe. That's all I want.

Just then, I hear keys rustling outside in the hall. Excitement shoots through me. I jump up from the couch and sprint to the door as quickly as my throbbing ankle and awkward gait will allow. I turn the knob and yank the door open.

"Jason!" I call out, but I only succeed in traumatizing my neighbor across the hall, who is trying to unlock her door. Her body flinches, and she spins to face me, her hand upon her chest. Her facial expression looks as though she thinks I am about to mug her.

"Oh, I'm so sorry," I say, throwing my palms up in front of my chest, feeling like an idiot.

The woman remains silent, giving me an untrusting look as she continues to fiddle with the doorknob while her eyes remain fixed on me.

Relax, lady; I'm not some psychopath.

The woman is tall and thin with long, jet-black hair, flowing down to the center of her back. Her cheekbones are very pronounced, casting a light shadow down her lower cheeks. Dark eyeliner is clumped across her lower rim, with a deep, purple eyeshadow brushed heavily on her eyelids.

"I didn't mean to startle you." I notice the woman's eyes narrow to a sliver as if she is assessing my genuineness. "I thought you were my boyfriend," I continue, trying to explain my enthusiastic outburst. "I'm Marney, by the way." I smile and point to the faded, brushed nickel digits on the outside of my door. "Apartment 3E."

The woman looks uncomfortable and nods, faking a smile as she manages to unlock her door. I continue to be my friendly self, though she seems to have no interest.

"Do you like it here?" I ask. "The previous tenant, Angie, seemed to like the apartment."

The woman cracks open her door and slips inside, replying, "Everything will be fine," before closing the door without any further conversation. I find her response odd, as much as I do the now yellow color of her door. She certainly likes to change things up. And quickly, too.

I slink back into my apartment, but not before gazing down the hallway toward the stairs for a last hope that I might see Jason's head bobbing into view. I don't.

Frustrated and feeling a headache coming on, I storm into the kitchen and dig into the cabinet drawer beside the fridge, where I know a bottle of Aspirin resides. I shake two into my palm and pause. It's been a while since I've dug into this stash, but I thought I remembered them being round instead of oval-shaped. Whatever. After the weird shit that's been going on with me lately, why would this be any different? Part of me thinks it's my memory playing tricks on me, another part screams to throw them away. I rationalize that I'm being paranoid.

I grab a glass from the overhead cabinet and fill it a quarter full from the drippy faucet.

Drip, drip, drip.

I pop the pills into my mouth and gulp the water down, then slide the bottom rim of the glass across my forehead. The cold, smooth surface offers soothing relief as I close my eyes and let the feeling ease my mind.

Things will be okay. You're not going crazy, Marney. You'll feel better when Jason gets home.

With that thought calming me, I open my eyes and breathe a heavy sigh. I go to place the empty glass in the sink, but bump the bottom edge against the corner of the counter. It slips from my fingers and drops to the floor. The glass shatters into pieces like the fragmented splinters of my life. An overwhelming feeling of despair comes upon me, and I want to break down and cry. I push it back to wherever it came from. I'm tougher than that and won't let it lead me down that path.

I squat to pick up the larger shards, each one reminding me that I need to be more careful; we can't afford new dishes. My eyes drift to the cabinet doors under the sink, and a memory floods my thoughts, distracting me. I feel something brush against my left shoulder. Before I can react, a rough hand covers my nose and mouth. My eyes fly open, and I instinctively kick my foot against the cabinet door, shoving my weight backward. I land hard on my ass and slide several inches, slamming my back against the opposite cabinets behind me before frantically swinging my head from side to side, my heart pounding to the beat of the drips.

Thump, thump, thump.

Drip, drip, drip.

Thump, thump, thump.

There's nobody here; only me. *What the fuck, Marney?*

Then I feel the burning sensation and look down at the red-stained piece of glass squeezed tightly in my grasp. I release my grip and watch the sharp glass slide from my shaky hand. Blood streams from the slice in my palm onto the floor, dribbling a steady cadence, much like the leaky faucet.

Drip, drip, drip.

Oh yeah, you're not going crazy or anything.

Chapter 17

The buzzing sound crashes into my skull as I thrust myself to a seated position on the bed, furiously fumbling to hit the button on my phone with my bandaged hand. Once I finally manage to turn the alarm off, I call out into the darkened room.

"Jason?"

Everything is quiet. The room is shrouded in dancing shadows as dawn begins to awaken through the curtains. I look at the time. 6:30. It's early. Why am I awake? I glance at the empty spot on the mattress beside me, the disheveled coverings clumped untidily in a heap like Jason was in a hurry this morning. The sheets are still warm. That should be a comfort to me. It isn't. The closet door is open, displaying his dangling shirts. That's not like him. He's much too organized not to close it.

"Jason, are you here?"

Silence.

As I stretch my arms to the ceiling and let out a yawn, it hits me like a freight train. It's Monday! I start my new job today. A smattering of nerves shoots through me, and I suddenly feel anxious and rushed. I toss the blanket off me and jump out of bed, wobbly, stumbling into the bathroom with only adrenaline keeping me upright. I turn the water on in the shower to let it warm up and then look at my frumpy self in the mirror. I'm draped in my standard sleeping attire: an oversized, white T-shirt and baggy shorts with my hair tangled in more clumps than the blanket. I crinkle my nose. *That's the epitome of beauty right there.*

I let out a sigh, stifling my sarcastic thoughts. The shower will work its magic, and makeup will do the rest. If that doesn't work, I can always resort to wearing a mask. The thought is amusing and puts a smile on my face as I peel my shirt off over my head. After I throw it to the floor and look back at myself in the steaming mirror, my smile fades, replaced with concern and fear.

"What the fuck?" I whisper, peering at my reflection as I twist my upper body and reach my hand across my stomach to my left side. My fingers glide across a large, darkened bruise at the bottom of my ribs that stretches onto my back. How did I do that? Did I sleep funny? What could have caused..?

Flashes of the night before pounce into my head. The shattered glass, the thought of someone grabbing me again, and my aggressive response by shoving myself backward. I hit my back pretty hard against the cabinet, but this? Holy shit! I look like I went one-on-one with a prizefighter. I shake my head, distraught. I look like a walking wound. Between the burns on my wrists, the cut on my ankle, the bruises on my arms and side, and the slice in my hand, I'm a damn poster for battered women. I'm falling apart.

Speaking of which..,

I pick at the packing tape that's been holding the folded toilet paper pressed against my injured palm. It peels away, tugging at my skin while I squint, peeking out of the side of my eye, squeamish about the expected sight of congealed blood hiding an infected wound. The tape releases, and the top of the makeshift 2-ply bandage falls free, dangling from the side of my hand. My eyebrows untuck, and I do a double-take to find there is no wound.

"What?" I say aloud, rubbing the fingers of my other hand along the crease lines of where the slice in my skin should be, but isn't.

I don't understand. I cut myself last night. I know I did. That's what the bandage was for.

I pull the flapping piece of tape and bathroom tissue up to look at it, but there's no blood. How can that be? I was bleeding. I didn't imagine that. This makes no sense.

I rip the remaining piece of tape off in frustration, wondering what is happening to me. I have to let Jason know when he gets home tonight. Am I sick? Is it the pregnancy? Is this sort of thing normal for expectant mothers?

No, Marney. Children drive their parents crazy after they're born, not before.

I'm glad I can still retain my humor in all of this, even though it's not a laughing matter. Maybe it's time to contact my doctor. Just what we need, yet another expense. It will have to wait. I have to get to work. I can't afford to lose my job before I've even begun. Besides, if I keep injuring myself, we'll need all the money we can get to cover the medical bills. Based on the frightening sight looking back at me, the chances of me paying with my good looks have dwindled from extremely unlikely to not a snowball's chance in Hell. My shoulders drop in defeat as I let out a huff. *Work it is.*

I ignore the peculiar anomalies plastering my skin and step under the soothing hot stream, scanning the tile walls for a soap message. It eludes me. It's not that I expect anything, but I thought Jason would have at least left me a good luck message. Today of all days. But, knowing him, he probably forgot about me starting at Tutter & Associates. And just like that, I already forgive the lovable lug. Of course, the hot water helps.

I squeeze all I can out of the shower, then wrap myself in a towel cocoon and wade out into the bedroom to retrieve some underwear. It doesn't immediately register until my hands are buried five layers deep in the stack of clothing on the dresser. The closet door is now closed. That was open when I went into the bathroom; I know it was.

"Jason?" I call out into the silence. "Are you still here?"

I wait and listen, but I don't hear anything except that infernal kitchen sink.

Drip. Drip. Drip.

I look at the closet door again. Did I close it? I must have. If Jason had been here, he would have said goodbye before he left. *Did* he say goodbye? I must have been half-comatose this morning when he got out of bed. *Right, sure, Marney. And apparently, while he was getting ready, and also when he left.* It's so weird; it seems like it's been days since I've seen him, but I just cleaned out his voicemail when he came home last night. And then he cooked dinner. We had.., um..,

Think, Marney. For Christ's sake, what the hell did he cook? Why is everything so hazy?

I glance over at my phone on the nightstand and purse my lips. It's not that complicated. I'll just call Jason and get all my questions answered at once.

I grab my phone and click on his number, tapping my foot impatiently as I listen to the rings. But then, the recorded voice, informing me that Jason is unavailable and that his inbox is full, stops my heart for a second. My chest tightens. How is that possible? I deleted all of his messages. I know I did. I did! Didn't I?

Chapter 18

My anxiety is sky high when I pull into Tutter & Associates' parking lot. I can't be concentrating on bruises and full in-boxes and crazy dreams when I need to focus on my new job. Mr. Tutter decided to take a chance on me; I can't let him down. I won't.

I park several spots away from the lamppost to preserve my sanity. I don't need another strange occurrence like the first time I was here. Confused or not, I know where I parked my car the last time. At least, I'm pretty sure I know where I parked.

I turn off the engine and take a deep breath, letting the nerves drain from me. Starting a new job is always stressful, but everything feels a little more out of sync of late. I've held off the morning sickness, but the hormones, the foggy memory, the injuries I've somehow sustained, it's all become too much. I just want to get in there and start working – to feel like I'm contributing to something again.

I look at myself in the rearview mirror and give myself some encouraging words.

"You can do this, Marney. It's like riding a bike."

Then, I realize I haven't ridden a bike since I was sixteen, and the nervous jitters return. I take in a deep, cool breath and let it out, nodding confidently to offer assurance to my worried mind.

I pull my keys from the ignition and exit the vehicle, lifting my chin confidently to remind myself that I deserve this job. I stride to the front door with a sense of determination. I *will* make an impact. I'll show Mr. Tutter he made the right decision when he hired me.

I step through the front door, and that strong smell of antiseptic hits my nose like someone just hosed the furnishings down with an extra-strength formula. I ignore the burning sensation in my nostrils and walk to the front reception desk, smiling politely at the woman seated in the chair. It's not the same woman who greeted me the first time. This one is older with an edgier appearance. She doesn't smile at all while I stand patiently, waiting for her to look up from her monitor to acknowledge me. When she does, she offers an annoyed glare like she doesn't appreciate being bothered.

"May I help you?" she says in that way that makes it feel like she doesn't *actually* want to help me.

"Hi. I'm Marney Fitzgerald. I'm starting to-day."

"Starting what, dear?"

The woman's tone is harsh and stings me for a second, but I keep my composure.

"Oh, I'm sorry," I answer. "I'm starting *here*; today's my first day. Mr. Tutter is expecting me."

"I see," she replies. "Just one moment, please."

The rude woman picks up the phone while keeping her eyes trained on mine, and presses a button. *Not a great start, Marney.*

"Hello, Mr. Tutter. There's a woman here in the lobby to see you. She says today is her first day. Okay. Very well."

The woman hangs up the phone and forces a smile in my direction.

"Mr. Tutter will be right out to see you."

"Thank you," I reply, maintaining my smile, though every ounce of me wants to jump over the desk and slap some courtesy into the woman. I re-frain. She's obviously not important enough to be kept in the loop.

I pull out my phone and turn away from the desk, pretending to check my messages so I don't have to see the old bat burning a hole through me with her stare. After a few minutes, which feels like an eternity, the door to the right of the reception desk swings open. A well-dressed, middle-aged bald man walks out. He's wearing nicely-pressed slacks and an olive-green sweater over a tan but-ton-up shirt with the collar folded over the sweater's neck. I see him glance at the receptionist as he points his finger in my direction. The receptionist nods. The man flashes a smile and extends his right hand.

"Hello, Miss..?"

"Fitzgerald," I answer, shaking his hand. "Marney Fitzgerald."

"So, what brings you to Tutter & Associates today?" he asks.

I look toward the still-open door, waiting for someone else to exit.

"I interviewed with Mr. Tutter last week, and he offered me a job. He asked if I could start on Monday, so here I am." I exaggerate my smile to show my enthusiasm. "Is Mr. Tutter here today?"

The man gives me a sideways glance before turning his head to the receptionist. When he turns back, he has a confused look on his face.

"I'm Mr. Tutter," he says.

My heart thumps heavily against my chest. I look to the open door again.

"Oh!" I let out. "I'm sorry. This is embarrassing." I grin awkwardly. "My interview was with an older gentleman. Your father, perhaps? His name was Jedidiah Tutter."

The man's eyes narrow. "Jedidiah was my father, yes, but you didn't interview with him last week."

I find his delivery rather rude, and I don't appreciate that he doesn't believe me.

"I did," I reply more sternly. "We were in the office just beyond that door, down the hall on the left. He said he appreciated my honesty, and he..,"

I freeze, just then thinking about the man's words.

"I'm sorry," I redirect. "Did you say, Jedidiah '*was*' your father?"

"That's right. My father passed away seven years ago."

"There must be some kind of mistake," I reply. "I was here last Wednesday. I interviewed with a white-haired gentleman for the bookkeeper position. I received paperwork."

"I believe you're right about there being a mistake," he says. "Unfortunately, Miss Fitzgerald, I believe it is *you* who are mistaken. We don't currently have a bookkeeper position available."

"But I was offered the job," I state. "I called on Thursday and accepted. I was told to start on Monday."

He offers me a concerned look. "I don't know who you spoke with in this office, but I'm sorry, there isn't a position."

"But I..," I look to the open door again, waiting for the big reveal, that this was all just a joke – the same joke played on every new employee. But instead, a different revelation hits me. There is no job. There was no interview. It's the same crazy nightmare as my other two visions. It isn't real. It was *never* real. I'm going insane.

"But I need this job, Mr. Tutter," I squeak out, sounding desperate.

"I'm so sorry," he replies. "I have nothing available."

My shoulders drop in defeat. My eyes burn. I want to cry, but I won't let myself. Not here.

"I understand," I mumble, dropping my chin to my chest. "Thank you for your time."

I don't bother shaking his hand a second time. Instead, I quietly turn and walk toward the exit.

Crushed.

Confused.

Unemployed.

Chapter 19

The tears erupt from my eyes the moment I get in my car. I can't believe this is happening. There is something seriously wrong with me. How could I have been so convinced I was starting a new job today, when it seems I didn't have an interview – at least, not one with the real Mr. Tutter. Or even someone from the living. Yet, it felt so real. It had to be. How else could I have known the senior Tutter's name? Jedidiah. I'd never even heard that name before my interview. Was someone playing a sick joke on me, posing as Old Man Tutter? Or was the whole thing all a fake, imaginary, all-in-my-head interview?

Out of frustration, I slam my palms against the top of the steering wheel and let out a piercing wail. What are we going to do? We were counting on this job. We need the money. Jason's salary alone can't keep us afloat much longer. He's going to be so disappointed when he hears the terrible news. Or maybe he'll be upset when he finds out there was never a job in the first place, and that his girlfriend is losing her mind. He's going to have me committed.

What now?

I angrily wipe the tears away with my sleeve, staring out the windshield at the building, the backlit Tutter & Associates sign taunting me about what could have been. I'm completely devastated. I need to find another job. And fast. I can't wait too long; nobody will hire a fat, pregnant woman who's about to burst.

Still upset, I jam my keys into the ignition and watch the damn cow dangle back and forth like it's a rocking horse. That should have been the end of it. I should have turned the key and started the car, and paid no attention to it. But it's like it's laughing at my misfortune. And because I am so focused on the creepy, swaying bovine, I notice the words coming from its mouth have changed.

"You're never pasture prime."

What? How can that be? I clamp onto the little metal cow mid-swing and rub my thumb over the embossed word balloon. It's only for a second, but when I remove my thumb, the phrase is back to what it should be: "I love moo." Of course. Why would I expect anything different? I've gone full-blown cuckoo. I shake my head and start the car; it's going to be a long ride back home.

Back at the apartment building, I sit quietly in my car, thinking of ways to break the news to Jason. None of them are pleasurable. I'll just come out and tell him it was all a mistake. He'll understand. He always does. Hell, he may not even remember it by tomorrow. Whether he does or doesn't, it's still going to sting in the moment. I'm not looking forward to letting him down. Again.

I step from my vehicle, this time less concerned with where I've parked. It doesn't matter; I've got nowhere to be. I slink in through the rear entrance and scuttle up the stairs to the third floor. When I turn the corner into the hallway, I see Toby in his denim overalls, sitting at the base of my apartment door, his bare feet crossed at the ankles, and his legs folded up to his chest with his forehead resting on his knees. He looks so small, so innocent. He's been waiting for me. Does he consider me a friend? That's adorable.

I walk heavily down the hall so he hears me coming. I don't want to scare the boy. It doesn't occur to me until I'm halfway to him that my ankle isn't bothering me as it had been. *Something is finally going right for a change.* Toby hears my footsteps and looks up from his knees, his unsmiling face showing little in the way of excitement. If he is happy to see me, I wouldn't know it.

"Hello there, Toby," I say with a smile. "Have you been waiting for me?"

He pushes himself up and slides to the side to allow me access to the doorknob.

"I wanted to make sure you were okay," he says. "You know, after what happened."

His comment takes me by surprise, and my brain immediately goes to my horrible experience at the accounting firm. But he can't possibly be talking about that.

"After what happened?" I question, my hand trembling as I fidget with my keys, searching for the right one. "What do you mean?"

"Nothing," he replies, watching me wrestle with my keyring. Then, he places his tiny hand on mine. "It's unlocked."

"What?" I stop struggling and look into his eyes. Something in them twists my insides. I look at the doorknob with uncertainty. Didn't I lock it? I grab the knob and give it a turn. The door cracks open. My tense shoulders drop as a feeling of disappointment washes over me. I could have sworn I locked it. I push the door open the rest of the way, and Toby invites himself in by swiftly stepping under my outstretched arm. He quickly makes his way to his favorite piece of furniture. Being the responsible adult and soon-to-be Mom, I have to ask.

"Are your parents okay with you being here?"

His legs begin to kick back and forth against the front of the chair.

Thump. Thump. Thump.

He remains silent, staring at me like he's curious about my every move.

"Oookay," I mutter under my breath while closing the door. As I turn to face him, I find it odd that the boy has worn the same blue overalls and striped shirt each time I've seen him. Are they his favorite? Does he have nothing else to wear? Then it dawns on me that perhaps the boy hasn't been honest with me. Could he be homeless? A runaway? I've never met his parents, and I'm still not sure where he lives. That would explain a lot.

"Toby, I don't mind you coming here, but I think I should meet your parents. They should at least know where you are, so they don't worry."

"They know," he responds.

"Do they?" I question. "Well, maybe you can tell me which apartment you live in, and I can stop by and say hello sometime."

"They don't like visitors. Not since..." The boy goes silent and stops kicking his heels into the chair. "They aren't home much," he continues.

The boy is tactical, I'll give him that. He doesn't cave under pressure. I traipse across the living room and place my keys on the dinette table next to...

The manila envelope I received from Tutter & Associates. The employment package. It's here. It's not all in my head. I *did* have an interview, and I *did* receive the benefits information. But then, what was that all about when I was there this morning? I don't underst...

"What was there?" the boy asks, interrupting my troubled thoughts.

"Wh-what?" I turn to see him pointing at the bare end table beside the couch. A shiver creeps up my arm at the sight. The framed photo of me and Jason at his brother's lake house is missing. Only a rectangular outline of dust remains where it once sat. I don't get it. Where is it?

I rush to the table and instinctively slide my fingers across the dusty surface, disturbing what was a perfect rectangle. I glance behind the table and between it and the couch to see if it has fallen to the floor. Distracted, I don't notice that Toby has gotten up from the chair until he is almost at the door. That's when I hear him whisper.

"He's not coming back."

That immediately snaps me around just as he is closing the door behind him. What did he say? I frantically run to the door to catch him, but when I open it, he is already gone.

His voice was soft, but I swear I heard him clearly. *He's not coming back.* Why would he say that? What did he mean by that? Who was he talking about? My eyes scan the silent, empty apartment, finally landing on the scattered remnants of dust on the end table.

"Jason?" I call out quietly, expecting no response.

Chapter 20

At first, it was the silence, so palpable, so heavy. The air was thick and stale, siphoning all sound from the apartment. Then, it was the ticking of the clock on the wall above the dinette table that held my senses captive.

Tick. Tick. Tick.

Every second, hammering into my skull, louder than the last until the sound was unbearable. It was even worse than the dripping faucet.

Drip. Drip. Drip.

Something is wrong; I can feel it. It isn't just the eerie words spoken by a child. *He's not coming back.* The apartment feels different, cold. Where are you, Jason?

The hours creep by. I spend my time divided between pacing a distinct figure eight across the living room floor and staring out the window, praying for Jason's truck to pull into the parking lot. Neither helps my already fragile state of mind. At some point, I drift off on the couch, waking at midnight to discover he still hasn't returned. I try his phone again. It goes straight to the recording before bouncing me off. I pace some more until the worry weighs too heavily on me, and I drag myself to bed. I try to sleep, but every time I close my eyes, I see his face. I hear his words. *There's something I've gotta take care of. I won't be out too long.*

Today, it's been too long.

At two a.m., I try his phone again. Nothing. I rub my hand across his side of the bed. It remains cold. Then, almost without thinking, my hand transitions to my stomach and swirls around my belly.

Please be all right, Jason.

I hear the door close, and my eyes snap open. I fell asleep. How could I have fallen asleep? For a second, I remain lying in bed, eyes wide, staring at the ceiling. Did I hear that? My hand compresses the comforter next to me. No Jason. I hold my breath, listening for any sound to permeate the darkness. I hear a step, a creak in the floorboards. It's him! I spring out from under the covers, nearly falling face-first off the side of the bed. Before I can catch myself, cold hands clasp onto my shoulders, saving me from hitting the floor. I gasp heavily just before the light flicks on, revealing my savior.

"Whoa! Easy there. You almost took a spill."

His voice penetrates through me, soothing and calm, wrapping around me like a safety blanket. He's here! He's come back! In less than a heartbeat, I latch my arms around him in a snug embrace, pressing my cheek against his muscular chest.

"Where have you been?" I ask, my eyes squeezed tightly shut. "I was worried sick. I didn't know if you were ever coming back. And then Toby made some comment, and you weren't answering your phone. And I didn't know where..."

"Hey, hey. Shhhhh. It's okay." I feel his hand stroke my hair at the back of my neck, and it gives me shivers. "Slow down. I'm here now."

"But where were you?" I question, still holding him tight.

"Don't worry about that. Let's think about now. I've got you, and I'm never letting you go."

"Promise?"

He pries me loose from our embrace and gently grips my upper arms, looking into my eyes with that sparkle that always makes me melt.

"I promise." He smiles with a devilish grin and backs me up until the back of my legs fold against the edge of the mattress, sitting me down. I offer him an amused, crooked smirk.

"What are you doing?" I ask playfully.

"It's been so long since I've held you, since I've felt you against me."

I feel a tingle between my legs as I surrender to his weight. He forces me onto my back and rubs his leg between my thighs, heightening my excitement. I reach up to unbutton his shirt, but he shoves my arms away, raising and lowering his eyebrows like he has a plan.

"Uh, uh. Not so fast," he says, wagging his index finger from side to side.

He leans forward, pressing his body onto mine. I hear my breathing shift and deepen as his lips caress the side of my neck. I don't struggle. I turn my head for easier access. His tongue tickles my earlobe, and I bite my bottom lip. I give away my anticipation with my quivers. When he's done teasing me, he pushes himself up and slides his hands down over the front of my shirt, slowing over my breasts on his way down. Even through the fabric, my erect nipples slide along his palms, letting him know how stimulated I am. When his hands get to my waist, he teases me further by slipping his fingers under the waistband of my shorts, letting them skim across my waistline.

"That's not fair," I whisper, squirming and gripping the blanket in my fists.

"Who said anything about being fair?" he replies. He pulls his hands from my shorts and snatches the bottom of my shirt. I anxiously await his next move, but he freezes. I open my eyes, wondering what he's waiting for, only to find he is no longer smiling. Instead, he has an angry grimace burned onto his face.

"Jason?" I push myself up onto my elbows. "What's wrong? Why did you stop?"

I watch his Adam's apple rise and lower along his neck as he swallows hard. He releases my shirt.

"Babe? What is it?" I question.

His eyes narrow. "Who's Toby?"

My eyes thrust open, and I jump to a seated position. The daylight shines in from the window, causing me to squint and put my hand up in front of my eyes. I look at the bed beside me. Empty. I scan the room for signs that Jason had been here, but I already know the answer. Jason didn't come home last night. It was all just a dream. Toby's words come barreling back into my head, and something about them hits harder today. *He's not coming back.*

Chapter 21

Morning brings more bruises. I'm almost not surprised to see them. The new spots along my shoulders are exactly where Jason grabbed me to prevent me from falling. I can *feel* the memory in my skin. Only he didn't grab me. He couldn't have. He never came home last night. So the bruises are as much a mystery as every other blemish on my white flesh.

I lean closer to the mirror, staring into my bloodshot eyes. How can all of this be happening? Why didn't Jason come home? He didn't even call. That isn't something he would neglect to do. My thoughts pull me in all the worst directions. Did he forget where he lived? With his brain injury, it's not a stretch to think he could be out walking the streets somewhere, confused. Maybe he placed his phone down somewhere and can't recall where? Did he.., did he decide to leave me? *Don't be ridi-*

culous, Marney. He's always looked out for me. Plus, all of his things are still here. No, this feels different. Even if he decided he wanted out of this relationship (lord knows he could have any woman he wants), he wouldn't walk out on his child. That's not who he is. I step back from the mirror to view my bare stomach and gently rub my hand over it. In that moment, the feeling comes upon me, and I spin toward the toilet, buckling to my knees. I heave, expelling only clear liquid from my mouth. I stay motionless, muscles clenched, my hair hanging dangerously close to the water's surface. I wait for a second bout, but it doesn't come. I wipe my palm across my lower lip to remove a dangling string of saliva, then swallow hard to ensure everything that wants to come up has. That's it for right now.

I force myself to my feet and flush the toilet, watching the water spiral down, down, down, like what my life has felt like recently. I glance into the mirror again, eyeing the new shoulder bruises.

Where the hell are you, Jason?

He's always communicated his whereabouts and whether he would be late. He didn't do that. Something is wrong, and it starts with that damn letter we received. It seemed threatening.

Did you think we wouldn't find you?

Whatever it was about, I know that's what Jason meant when he said he had something to take care of. He probably didn't want me to know. He knew I'd worry. Ha! Look at me now. And why shouldn't I worry? He's been missing for...how long has it been? A day? Two days? I don't even know anymore.

I rap my knuckles on the vanity countertop and purse my lips. I'm not going to sit here and wonder what might have happened. I'm going to do something about it. I'm going to find Jason. I storm out of the bathroom without a thought of my appearance. I grab the first shirt from the top of the clothes pile and throw it over my head. Next, I slide a pair of sweatpants over my shorts and march into the living room, where I scoop up my keys and the mysterious letter from the table. I slip on my shoes, take a glance around the apartment, making sure I'm not forgetting anything, then yank the door open. I immediately stammer back at my neighbor's presence, standing outside my door. I can tell she is taken aback as well, as her eyes thrust open, and her fisted hand, which was ready to knock, swings back to her side.

"Oh, I'm sorry," the woman begins. "It's Marie, isn't it?" she asks.

"Marney," I correct her.

"Marney. Right. I'm horrible with names."

Maybe if you'd paid attention when I tried being neighborly and introduced myself.

"I don't mean to bother you," she continues, "but you seemed pretty distraught last night, and I thought I'd check in with you to see how you were doing."

"What?" I question. My heart rate begins to increase.

"I imagine you *would* be confused," she responds. "After the way I found you wandering the halls last night when I got home from work. You didn't look in any condition to be out and about."

"Wait. I was...wandering the halls last night?" I bring my hand to my forehead and rub furiously, trying to recall what happened.

"You don't remember me walking you back to your door?" she questions, her eyes squinted. "You kept telling me that Jason...that is your boyfriend's name, right? Well, you kept saying he was gone and that you didn't know where he was."

"I'm sorry," I say, shaking my head. "I don't remember any of this. Was I really out here walking around?"

"Yeah. And you were quite upset."

"I...I don't remember. Th-thank you for telling me. I hope I wasn't too much trouble."

"Not at all. I'm just glad to see you're looking better this morning."

"Um, yeah," I nod. "I'm feeling much better, thank you." *Except for the part about Jason still being gone, and me learning I'm sleepwalking in the middle of the night.*

"Well, if there's anything I can do..." The neighbor pauses and smiles.

"No, thank you. You've done more than enough. I appreciate you checking in on me."

"Of course."

The woman turns and steps through the open door of her apartment. Just before she closes it behind her, I call out, "I didn't get your name."

Her complexion instantly changes, and she stares at me with a deadpan expression on her face. Her eyes are now cold and dark as she nudges the door closed to within a few inches, where only a sliver of her face remains visible.

"The leaves are beautiful this time of year," she says, before closing the door the rest of the way.

At first, the words cause my gut to churn, as if something inside me shook loose. Then, the feeling subsides just as quickly. I shake my head in confusion. *What the hell was that?* I ask for her name, and she answers with some random phrase. It's weird. This entire situation. Everything. I can't believe I was wandering around out here. I don't remember that. Why can't I remember? What the fuck? Whatever. It's not important right now. What *is* important is finding out where Jason is. I have to make sure he's all right.

I clench my fingers tightly and crinkle the letter I'm holding. I close my apartment door, jostle the handle to ensure it's locked, and hastily stride to the stairwell. I'm halfway down the second flight before I notice how well my ankle is holding up, like the adrenaline rush is suppressing the pain. *It's about time*, I think. It's been days.

I get to the bottom floor and push open the rear door facing the parking lot. Outside, the daylight hurts my eyes as the sun beats down across the first row of cars, its glare reflecting off several windshields. Even with the sun's heat, the air is crisp and burns the insides of my nostrils as I inhale. A subtle breeze from the west passes over me, causing my arm hairs to pull at my skin, making me realize I didn't grab a jacket. Oh well.

I unlock my car and hop inside, away from the morning chill. I place the letter on the passenger seat and start the car, just as that creepy Mr. Jeffries exits the building. I try to duck down to hide behind the steering wheel, but he sees me and locks his eyes in my direction. I lower the sun visor to give even less visibility into my windshield, but he continues his perverted stare. I can't deal with this. I start the car and pull away, ignoring the man as his head follows my vehicle.

I don't have time to be a part of that twisted man's sexual fantasy. Jason is out there somewhere. He needs help. I've got to get to the police station and show them this letter. They'll understand once I tell them. They'll figure it out. They have to.

They have to.

Chapter 22

The police station looks intimidating as I pull into a spot along the right side of the building, its narrow, tinted windows stitched between columns of cold brick and mortar. My eyes follow a crack along the exterior façade that extends down from the roof like a lightning bolt, weaving a diagonal path that splinters in three directions near the foundation. Like my life, it's slowly crumbling for all to see. It's only a matter of time before it all falls apart, a harsh reminder that everything eventually gives way.

I shrug away my disparaging thoughts, swipe the letter from the seat, and exit my driver's side door with determination. I practically bound up the concrete slab steps to the entrance, where an exiting officer holds the door open for me. I thank him and step up to a large glass partition with a dozen or so tiny holes for a person to speak through. A female officer behind the window looks up and notices me.

"May I help you, ma'am?"

What is with everybody calling me "ma'am"?

"Hi, is there someone I can speak with about filing a missing person's report?"

"Is this person a relative?" she asks.

"No, he's my..."

"Child or adult?" she interrupts.

"Adult. It's my boyfriend."

"Can I get his name?"

"It's Jason Leery," I reply. "He didn't come home..."

"And how long has Jason been missing?" the officer interjects again, writing notes on a lined pad.

"Well, it's...it's only been since yesterday, I think, but he..."

"So, it's only been twenty-four hours?" she questions, looking at me as if that's not long enough to matter.

"I...I think so."

"You think so?"

"I'm not really sure," I tell the officer. "I've been losing track of time lately. It might be long-er."

"Losing track of time?" the officer repeats in a slow, steady manner, like she's doubtful. "So, it could be less than twenty-four hours, then?"

"No! I mean, yes, it could be slightly less, but he didn't come home last night, and I haven't been able to get in touch with him."

The female officer huffs. "Ma'am, I appreciate..."

"Stop calling me ma'am!" I raise my voice. "Jesus Christ! You don't understand. Jason never stays out, and if he were to, he would contact me. He has a brain injury. He sometimes has memory issues because of a concussion he sustained. I'm afraid he might be lost somewhere and doesn't know how to get home." My voice trembles. "He's out there alone, maybe hurt or who knows what else. You need to take this seriously. I'm telling you..,"

"Okay, take it easy, ma'am. I mean, miss. I know you're worried right now, and I *get* that. How old is your boyfriend?"

"He's twenty-eight."

"Well, please don't take this the wrong way, but is it possible that he just needed to get away for a while. You know.., to get some air?"

I give her a nasty look. How could I not take that the wrong way?

"I'm sorry," she continues, "but we have to ask the questions, even if they're not pleasant. Could he be at a friend's house or maybe with a family member?"

"No, it's not that; he doesn't have any family around here, and the friends he has.., well, he would have contacted me."

"I sympathize with you," the officer states. "I really do." She pauses and lets out a breath. "Listen, I know you don't want to hear this, but in my experience, when a man doesn't come home for the night, it usually means he…"

"No!" I stop her mid-sentence. "Jason wouldn't do that to me. He wouldn't. We're having a baby; I'm pregnant."

"Congratulations," the officer says with a half-hearted smile.

"You don't understand," I continue. I lift the letter I've been holding into view. "You see, we received this threatening letter, and when Jason left, he said he had to take care of something. I think he went to look for whoever dropped off this letter."

"A threatening letter? Can you slide it under the glass, please?"

She points to a round, bowl-shaped recess in the counter at the base of the glass. I slide the folded letter across as she had asked. She unfolds it and reads the words, narrowing her eyes.

"You see?" I tell her. "There must be a connection."

She lifts her eyes from the paper and tucks her eyebrows together.

"Miss, this is a grocery list."

She turns the paper so I can see.

Milk.

Eggs.

Coffee.

Bread.

My mouth hangs open while I try to process what I'm seeing.

"No, that's not right," I say. "That's not what it said. I must have grabbed the wrong paper. It said, 'Did you think we wouldn't find you?'"

"This certainly doesn't say that," the woman officer says cynically, sliding it back under the glass.

"You have to believe me," I plead. "There *is* a letter. Someone threatened us. I just grabbed the wrong paper. Jason is in danger. I can feel it. You have to do something. He needs your help!"

"Calm down. Calm down. Here's what I'm going to do. Let me take down your name and number."

"My name is Marney Fitzgerald." I pull out my phone and place the display against the glass. "Here's my number."

She takes note of it on the same pad with her other scribblings. "And do you have a recent picture of your boyfriend?" she asks.

"Yeah, right here on my phone." I open my photo library and begin scrolling through the pictures. A few seconds go by with no success. The officer jumps in.

"You can always come back and drop one off."

"No, I've got some," I reply. "Just a moment." I continue to scroll and scroll, but can't seem to find any pictures of Jason. I know they're in here. I took some of him early last week when he was trying to kill a spider in the bathtub. He was more terrified of the thing than I was. But now it's not here. Why can't I find it?

"Miss, it's okay," the officer states. "I'll get all of this on file. If we hear anything in the next day or two, we'll give you a call."

"A day or two?" I question.

"Meanwhile," she jumps in, ignoring my concern, "I suggest you contact some of his friends or colleagues. Maybe they know where he is. If you still haven't heard anything by tomorrow night, come on back, and we'll go over the report in more detail. My name is Officer Poole." She reaches up to her chest and tugs at a little gold name tag with her name, "L. Poole" engraved on it.

"So, there's nothing you can do right now?" I question, my eyes watering.

"It's like I said," she answers. "He's an adult; he could have decided to stay out somewhere. Go home. Try not to worry too much. I'm sure everything will be fine."

Officer Poole nods confidently and offers me a warm grin. It isn't the outcome I had hoped for, but it's all I've got, and I have no choice but to accept it. I take the paper from the counter and stare at the list of items written in Jason's handwriting. How did I grab the wrong paper? It was right there on the table. Shit.

I crumple the paper into a tight wad, shove it in my pocket, and solemnly walk out of the police station, feeling worse than I had when I walked in. Everything seems to be going from bad to worse.

No sooner do those thoughts slip from my mind than I reach the bottom step and turn to face the parking lot.

"What the fuck?" I blurt.

Suddenly, things have gone from worse to worse-*er*.

My car has disappeared again.

Chapter 23

I storm back up the steps and burst through the precinct doors like I'm on fire, which catches the attention of the officer behind the glass - a man this time. *Wow, they change quickly*, I think. He gives me a side-eyed glare as I approach, and he nonchalantly reaches one hand up to the radio clipped to his shoulder like I'm a possible threat. When I reach the glass, I notice his eyes subtly glance down at my chest before coming back up to meet my annoyed stare.

"Are you all right, miss?" he asks. "Are you in some kind of trouble?"

I find it an odd question.

"Trouble? No," I say slowly.

"Are you hurt? Did somebody do that to you?"

"Wh-what are you talking about?" I ask. "Do what? I'm here about my car."

"Your shirt and, ah..," he waves his fingers near his cheek, "your face."

I pull back from the window and look down. My shirt has streaks of dried mud mixed with smeared blood across it. I brush my hand over it, and a sprinkling of dirt falls to the floor.

"What the hell?" I whisper.

I look up at the officer, who is giving me a concerned gaze. Then, I look to my left, where a display cabinet showcasing name tags of retired officers stands, its rear wall a mirror. I step up to it to get a glimpse of my face. My lower lip drops, and my eyes spring open in shock. I bring my left hand up to rub the scrape marks along my cheek and feel the warm, sticky liquid from the fresh wound. I reel and wince as my skin burns from the touch. I continue to stare, noticing my lower lip quivering, until the officer grabs my attention.

"Miss, were you in an accident?"

I swing my head around to face him. "N-no. Not an accident. I actually don't know what happened. I didn't realize..." I pause for a moment, not knowing how to continue. It doesn't make sense. How would anybody understand when I don't understand it myself? "I'm fine," I continue, stepping back up to the glass. "It must have been when I tripped up the stairs."

A look of doubt washes over the officer's face. Nevertheless, I focus on why I am here.

"I came in here, well, I was in here a few minutes ago, speaking with the other officer that was here, and she…"

"The other officer?" he questions, narrowing his eyes.

"Officer Poole," I nod. "She took down some infor…"

"I'm the only officer up front today, miss," he interjects. "Did you come in on another day?"

"No. No, it was just a few minutes ago. She was here, right where you are now."

"I see," he says. "I think we should get someone out here to take a look at you. You may have hit your head when you fell."

"What? No. I don't need anyone to look at me. I told you, I'm fine. There was another officer here."

"And what did you say the officer's name was again?" he asks.

"It was Poole," I answer. "L. Poole was on her little name tag."

"Poole?" he questions. "Well, there is no officer by that name who works here, and we don't wear little name tags on our shirts anymore." He points to an embroidered name above his shirt pocket. *T. Henderson.* Then, he points to the display cabinet. "We haven't worn them in years now."

I swivel and throw a glance at the cabinet. "But she…" I stumble for the words as I ease myself closer to the display again. "I swear, I'm not making this up." I look at all the name tags neatly lined in several rows, scanning through the names. Then, I see it. Seventh row, fourth tag in. L. Poole. My heart quickens.

"Miss, you hang tight. I'm going to have a paramedic take a look at you," the officer says, reaching for the radio clipped to his shirt.

"No!" I raise my voice. "I said I was fine." I quickly turn and run out the doors into the crisp air. I bend over and support myself by pressing my palms to my knees while trying to catch my breath. How can this be possible? I don't understand. I spoke with that female officer. She was here. But... her name tag was in that display case in a row labeled 1987.

Chapter 24

Everything shifts around me. The landscape twists and contorts, warping and bending, disorienting me. Buildings and signs sway and mash together, blurring the scenery between the familiar and the unrecognizable. The sounds of the city-the people, the cars-distort and fade, then rush back to me at once, clamoring in my skull. It's too much to take, and I almost collapse to the sidewalk under the unforgiving weight. Shaken, I squeeze my eyes shut, trying to ignore the uninterrupted pulse, to calm the raging storm wreaking havoc in my brain. I press my palms to my ears, hoping to sedate the perpetual static. I don't know what is happening. I don't know what is happening. I don't know what...

Wait. The change is almost immediate, like the flip of a switch. It's quiet. Almost unnervingly so. Silence permeates my being. I open my eyes, and everything around me resumes. The city reverts to its natural state. The air is calm but cool against my skin, the streets alive with a resonating flow. All is as it should be.

Except my car. It's still gone.

After everything that's been happening with me lately, I'm beginning to doubt if it was even here in the first place. But then, how did I get here? Did I walk? My shirt is a mess, my face scraped up. Perhaps I *did* fall like I told the officer inside. Maybe I hit my head, and that's why I can't remember. My God, I'm becoming as bad as Jason.

Jason! That's why I am here. Maybe he's home now. I pull my phone from my pocket and dial his number. Please, please answer.

"Hello?"

A man's voice, but not Jason's.

"Hello. Who is this?" I ask.

"Hey, you called me, lady," he replies. *"Who the fuck are you?"*

I pull the phone from my ear and check that I've dialed correctly. It's Jason's name and number on display, but it's not Jason on the other end.

"Where's Jason?" I blurt. "What are you doing with his phone?"

The man doesn't answer, but he's still on the line. His heavy breathing gives him away.

"Who are you?" I repeat angrily, my hand squeezing the phone. "What have you done with Jason? Where is he? Why did you answer his phone?"

There is silence at first, sending my thoughts scrambling. Then the man speaks up.

"Did you think we wouldn't find you?"

Then the phone goes dead.

My heart pounds.

"Hello? Hello?" I scream into the phone. Nothing. I frantically dial Jason again, but this time, there is no answer, and it kicks me off when it clicks over to voicemail. Fuck! Fuck! That was the guy, the person who left us the letter. *Did you think we wouldn't find you?* That's what he said. I reach two fingers into my pocket to pull out the crumpled ball of paper before I remember that there isn't anything on it except breakfast foods.

Shit! The real one is at the apartment.

What do I do? I can't go back into the police station. The officer already thinks I'm crazy. Hell, *I* think I'm crazy. Going back in will only make it easier for him. But Jason needs me. I've got to figure things out, get back to the apartment. It's only a few blocks. The walk will do me good; help me clear my head. Once I think this through, I'll know what to do. I'll come back with the correct letter after I've cleaned myself up.

The second block smells of smoke. Sirens in the distance tell of a fire not too far away. A school bus rumbles past. Every face in the windows looks like Jason's for half a second and then isn't. I quicken my pace.

As I near a small forested park, the smell changes to pine and wet leaves. It's a smell I used to love but have since learned to loathe. Still, the scent invades my nostrils without consent. I walk faster to get beyond the stink, but it stays with me. I close my eyes and scrunch my nose. It's only for a second, but when I reopen them, I'm no longer on the sidewalk. Instead, I'm in the middle of a forest with no buildings in sight. All around me are trees and leaves and more trees.

"What the..? Where am I?"

I spin in place, the leaves rustle underfoot.

"How did I get here?" I ask aloud as if the trees will somehow answer back. Nervously, I reach for my phone, tapping the back of my sweatpants before realizing they don't have rear pockets. I dig my hands into my front pockets. I feel my heart thud against the inside of my ribs. No phone.

Shit! I must have dropped it.

Panicking, I yank my hands free. The crumpled paper spills out onto the forest floor. I squat and feverishly shuffle my hands through the leaves, searching for my phone. Then I hear it. A voice in the distance. Soft at first. I can't make out what was said. I stand and look behind me, where I think the voice was coming from. I hear the voice again, a man's voice, this time closer, louder.

"I'm telling ya, she went this way."

I want to scream for help, but something inside tells me to stay quiet. My heart is beating like a drumline solo. That voice. There is something familiar about it, something that makes my skin crawl. I remain frozen, still, until I hear a twig snap, and something in my head yells at me.

RUN, MARNEY! RUN!

As fast as my legs can carry me, I run deeper into the labyrinth of trees, away from the voice. Leaves draped across the landscape are violently thrust aside by each hurried footstep. My breathing is shallow, my lungs on fire. I don't know where I am running to or why, only that I must put distance between me and the voice. I sprint faster, letting adrenaline carry me onward.

Have I run far enough? Is there anyone behind me? I turn my head to glance over my right shoulder to ensure I am still alone. I see only a vast expanse of forest, the ground blanketed in colorful, wet leaves. I think I am safe until I turn my head back and am met viciously by an oak tree's low-hanging limb. The thick branch slams into my face. My feet fly out from under me, and my back crashes hard against the ground, knocking the wind out of me.

I'm looking up at a darkening sky, the treetops blurry. I can't tell if it is the trees that are dancing or my eyesight that hasn't adjusted yet from the impact. I try to inhale, but the back of my throat scoffs and wheezes instead. I manage a slight groan and roll myself onto my stomach. I don't know how far I've run, but I know I can't stay where I am.

I press my forearm into the ground in front of me and muscle myself forward a few inches. My right foot joins the effort, the toe of my shoe digging into the soil. My other arm lurches forward, then my left leg. I crawl along the dirt and leaves until I am safely out of sight behind the large oak that assaulted me. I sit upright, my legs extended in front of me, pressing my back to the rough bark, my mind focused on breathing. I look down at my shirt decorated in brown. My tongue scrapes along the inside of my cheek, and I feel a backlash of pain rip through me. I bring my hand up to my cheek, gently wipe away the trickling blood, and smear it across the front of my shirt. Then, I hear the crunching of leaves from somewhere behind me.

My eyes skittishly dart left and right while I slowly slide my legs into me, taking care not to make noise. I hear more rustling leaves and the not-so-subtle thumping of footsteps.

Thump.

Thump.

Thump.

I can tell from the sound that there's more than one of them. A man's voice erupts.

"Here, kitty, kitty. We've got some treats for you."

It sounds like he's ten feet from me, and I now realize where I've heard that voice before.

I bearhug my trembling knees to my chest and close my eyes. If I can't see them, they can't see me. Isn't that how it works? The dreadful answer comes a second later.

"There you are, you troublesome, little bitch. Did you think we wouldn't find you?"

I open my eyes just a sliver to see a dirty hand waving a crumpled grocery list in front of my face. Tears form in my eyes just as a labored, stuttered breathing returns to me. I hear the click of a hammer cock back, like the sound my dad's revolver would make when he used to take me shooting as a little girl. I squeeze my eyelids shut as tight as they can go, thinking of Jason and our child. And then, the deafening sound explodes in my ears, disturbing the calm night.

Chapter 25

The cawing of the crows vacating the trees in a mass exodus is a welcoming sound. I'm still alive. My eyes spring open. It's still light out. I'm back on the sidewalk. The cars pass by, oblivious to the harrowing experience I've just encountered.

What *did* I encounter?

I quickly pat my hands over my body to make sure I am solid and not some form of a residual spirit, floating aimlessly in the wild. Or, perhaps, checking for a bullet wound. I gulp saliva down, looking at the treeline along the periphery of the park. I'm back. But, back from where? What the fuck was that? I was lost. Alone. Being chased. What is happening to me?

Instinctively, I look behind me to check if someone is following me. The sidewalk is empty, barren. I'm alone. This time, the word doesn't sound as frightening. Only sad. I turn forward and continue my walk back to the apartment.

The trip is longer than I expected, and I feel a twinge in the back of my ankle like the wound has reopened. As I pass by Mansfield's Market, I stop to allow my ankle some rest. The door to the small grocery shop is propped open with a little rubber wedge. When I look in, I see an older man beyond the center display of soft drinks. He's in a policeman's uniform, and he's smiling and waving in my direction. I turn my head to look behind me, thinking he must be waving at someone else, but there is nobody there. When I look back, the officer is gone. Instead, Mr. Mansfield is standing in the doorway, greeting me with his inviting smile.

"Marney!" he excitedly greets, his cheeks rosy red, his arms open wide like he's looking for a hug. "It's so good to see you. You look tired this morning."

"Just restless, I guess," I respond reflexively.

He chuckles. "Young people never sleep."

I flash a grin to be polite, but everything in me feels the opposite. I want to scream.

"Can I interest you in coffee?" he asks.

"Oh, uh, no. That's not necess…"

"Perhaps something else then? You know, milk, eggs, coffee, bread," he adds.

A chill runs down my spine. "What did you say?" I ask.

Mr. Mansfield's facial expression sours, his eyebrows tuck.

"I think you heard what I said, Marney.

"Milk.

"Eggs.

"Coffee.

"Bread."

My hands begin to shake, and my fingertips go numb. My feet begin to stumble sideways, carrying me away as I respond.

"I-I can't, Mr. Mansfield." I almost trip over my feet as I turn in the direction I'm headed. "I can't."

My stride lengthens, my pace quickens-anything to get back to the apartment faster. Why would Mr. Mansfield ask me that? Why *those* items? I slide my left hand into my pocket and feel the balled-up paper. It's still with me. I didn't drop it. How did he know?

I clear my head of it when I feel my stomach churn. I'm going to be sick again. I hasten my steps, turning them into an uncoordinated sprint, feeling every motion as the back of my pant leg slides up and down over the reopened gash in my ankle.

By the time I reach the apartment parking lot, I am out of breath and wishing for a walker. My lungs burn as much as my ankle, and stomach bile is creeping up into my throat. I rush past the line of cars against the rear of the building, noticing my vehicle is not among them.

Shit! Where the hell is my car?

I hurry up the rear staircase to the third floor and pause at the top of the stairs, looking down the hallway to my door. Something is different. Off. The carpeting is new. New color, new pattern. Lots of oranges and reds, reminding me of the forest floor, the colorful leaves blanketing everything in sight. I step forward, hearing the crunching and crackling under the weight of each step. I know it isn't possible, but it's there. I hear each sound, every subtle snap, giving away my location.

Crunch.

Crunch.

Crunch.

And then I feel it. A presence behind me, causing me to stiffen before I reach my door. My heart races, and I spin around quickly, poised to fight, my fists clenched, ready for battle.

A knot loosens between my shoulder blades when I see Toby, standing by the staircase, his eyes sad, his face cheerless.

"Toby!" I express, with both surprise and relief.

He slowly walks toward me, his bare feet gliding softly across the carpet, the sound of leaves a dissipating memory.

"I don't think this is a good time, Toby," I say, as the boy continues forward, unswayed by my tone. "I'm not feeling well." I keep focused on him as he approaches, his silent, somber stare eating away at my resolve, until he is right in front of me. He reaches out with his left hand and places his palm on my right hand, which I hadn't realized was still in a tense fist.

"It's okay, Marney," he whispers. "Let it go. Everything will be all right."

Something in the boy's words washes over me, and my muscles relax. My fist loosens, and my fingers open. Toby looks down and gently traces his fingers along the divots in my palm where my nails had dug in. He mingles his fingers with mine to hold my hand, and my breathing immediately calms. I can't help but feel, like me, the boy is alone. I push through the sorrow and force a smile.

"Thank you, Toby," I tell him, as he stares up at me with despondent eyes. "I feel better now." And I do. The urge to throw up has left me. "Would you like to come in? I have Jell-O."

He nods while his fingers twitch at the back of my hand. He's anxious to get out of the hall. With my empty hand, I feel for my keys but can't locate them. Before panic sets in, Toby squeezes my hand to get my attention.

"It's unlocked," he says.

"What?" I question, narrowing my eyes. The door can't be unlocked; I remember locking it. I reach for the door, doubtful the knob will turn, but it does. My first thought is that Jason made it home. I swing the door open and call his name.

"Jason?"

A rush of cool air douses me. The lights are off; the heat is off. No Jason. Toby releases my hand and storms into the apartment, darting for the chair. I step inside and close the door, feeling the harsh reality of my surroundings. Jason hasn't come home. Still, I glance around the apartment to see if anything has been disturbed. I notice my keys on the dinette table beside a piece of paper, and I shake my head, frustrated that I can be so absent-minded. I walk over to grab them and spot the words on the paper.

Did you think we wouldn't find you?

An image of a man's dirty hand flashes before me, his voice echoing in my ears, penetrating to my core. I close my eyes and pinch the bridge of my nose. *Get out of my head!*

Then everything is quiet again, except the ceaseless dripping from the kitchen faucet.

Drip.

Drip.

Drip.

As difficult as it is, I ignore the sound and reach for my keys. The cow offers me little comfort, and the word balloon from its mouth, which has changed again, even less. This time it reads, "Now you're milking it." I gasp in disbelief and drop them to the floor. Swallowing heavily, I glance over at Toby, worried that I might have scared him. He sits, unaffected by my sudden reaction, staring blankly at the bedroom door.

Of course, when is he ever ruffled?

I bend down to pick up the keys and notice the words have reverted to "I love moo." I can't explain it. I don't try. I snatch them up and stuff them into my pants pocket. When I look back at Toby, his gaze is still fixed on the bedroom door, like a puppy that senses something behind it. *Jason?*

To quash any uncertainty, I let the boy's undisrupted attentiveness convince me to check. I quickly open the door as my heart beats three times in one second. I wanted to believe that Jason would be inside, rolled up under the blankets, sleeping, but it's just another cold, empty room.

I'm about to shut the door when I notice the bottom drawer of the dresser is open. It's where Jason keeps his pants. Curious, I stride over to the dresser to find the drawer empty.

"Oh no," I whisper. "No, no, no, no no."

Frantically, I tug each drawer open-all of them empty-including the top drawer, mine, which held my socks and underwear. Hysterical, I twist toward the closet door and yank it open. It's full of my clothes, hanging from the rod, but none of Jason's. He's been here. He must have come while I was at the police station. That officer was right-Jason has left me. He's packed all his clothes and gone. How could he do that to me? To *us?*

I look down at the base of the closet and spy an old, zipped duffel bag, full and rounded. I don't remember that being there.

From the living room, I hear Toby's heels thud against the front of the chair.

Thump.

Thump.

Thump.

My jaw clenches, and I scrunch my face, hearing that man's footsteps on the hard forest ground.

Brushing it off, I pull the bag from the closet floor and swing it onto the bed, curious about its contents. Its torn seams burst a little, threads splaying from the gaps.

Thump.

Thump.

Thump.

"I don't really like it when you do that, Toby," I yell into the living room. "Can you please stop?"

I fight with the stuck zipper until it gives, and pull the worn flaps apart. My heart sinks into my chest. Pictures. Framed pictures of Jason and me. I dig into the bag, removing each of them one at a time. Some I recall, some are a mystery to me, memories of things that have never happened.

Then the thumping again.

Thump.

Thump.

Thump.

"Toby, please!" I yell. "Don't do that."

I dig deeper into the bag, and then freeze when my hand latches onto something square and fuzzy. I pull it out to see what it is, a small, felt-covered jewelry box - the kind that would hold a ring or a pair of earrings. I grab the hinged lid to open it when the incessant thumping from Toby's swinging legs belts out even louder.

Thump.

Thump.

Thump.

Annoyed, I slam the jewelry box down on the mattress and stomp to the bedroom door.

"I said stop!" I yell, peering out into the living room, aiming my anger at an empty chair. Toby is gone, the front door left wide open from where he ran out.

Chapter 26

I stand at the foot of the bed, biting my lower lip to prevent myself from biting my nails, while I stare at the little black box surrounded by picture frames scattered across the mattress, telling unfamiliar tales. I begin to pace, wondering what it all means-the pictures of untold stories, the jewelry box, packed away in a duffel bag at the bottom of our closet. It wasn't there before.

I step up to the side of the bed and swipe my fingers across the glass of one of the framed pictures, clearing away three paths of dust. In it, Jason and I are standing at the foot of a cliff, overlooking a sprawling town in the distance, his arm around me, his dimples exploding. We're both wearing hats that say "I Lovermont" across the front with a red heart in place of the first o. We look happy. The problem is, it can't be us. We've never been to Vermont. And Jason wouldn't be caught dead wearing a hat. He doesn't even like me rubbing my fingers through his hair, like I'm going to mess his perfectly groomed locks.

I don't understand any of this. Where did these pictures come from? They must be fake, though I recognize the ones of us posing in front of the Christmas tree in our old apartment. That seems like forever ago. The others..? I'm so confused. Who put them here and why?

My eyes redirect to the jewelry box, and a chill passes through me. I hesitate to open it, wondering why it was hidden away in an old duffel bag. I can't put it off any longer. Nervously, I snatch the box from the bed, and immediately, my hands begin to shake uncontrollably. I tell myself to stop, but it's like there is a broken link between my brain and my hands, and they're acting on their own impulses. I try to steady them by squeezing them to my chest, but it's pointless. I close my eyes and take a slow, deep breath to calm myself. The trembling slows but doesn't stop. It feels like a minor win.

I open my eyes and hold the box at arm's length, running different scenarios in my head. What if it's a ring? What if it's an *engagement* ring? Was I supposed to find it? What if I wasn't? Should I even know about it? Was Jason going to ask me to marry him? Maybe he wanted to surprise me with it. It's too late now. Curiosity has my ear, and it's whispering to me.

Open it.

Open it!

I grab the lid with my other hand and slowly crack it open. My heart flutters for an instant when the sparkle catches my eye. It's the most beautiful diamond I've ever seen. It must be at least a carat. How could Jason have afforded such a thing?

I don't get the chance to think about it further, as a sharp pain shoots through my side, buckling me. I drop the jewelry box, which bounces off the mattress to the floor, and I press my hands to my side to dull the pain. When I pull them away, blood is dripping from my palms. Wide-eyed, I look at my shirt. The fabric is wet, a ring of red spreading around a hole. The sight somehow makes the pain more palpable. I place my hand over the bloody hole and wince as I stumble my way to the bathroom and flip on the light. I slowly lift my shirt to get a look in the mirror at what I am dealing with and cringe at the sight.

Blood trickles from a hole in my side. In a panic, I grab the towel hanging from the towel bar and use it to compress against the wound. Blood stains the white cotton as the sting forces my eyes closed. Images spark in my mind. A dirty hand holding a crumpled piece of paper. The clicking sound of a gun. My breath shortens, and I become rigid. And then, the earsplitting sound of a gunshot jolts my eyes open. I gasp, catching my breath as I stare at myself in the mirror. My eyes drift down to the towel bunched at my side. There's no more red creeping into the stitching. Mumbled words escape my quivering lips.

"What? How?"

I slowly peel the towel back, exposing my skin. The hole is gone, but the large bruise is still present, a dull blue in the center, greenish-yellow at the edges. I gently place my palm against it. The spot is sensitive and warm to the touch. Beneath my fingertips, something pulses, like a heartbeat that isn't mine. Startled, I pull my hand away, and my shirt drops back down. Was that a kick? Did my baby just..? It couldn't have been. I'm only six weeks along. It's my mind playing tricks on me, a phantom kick. I'm sure all expectant mothers go through this sort of thing.

Right, Marney. You keep telling yourself that. Maybe one of these days you'll believe it.

I gaze at myself in the mirror, taking in my appearance. My shirt is whole, no blood. I look exhausted. No wonder I'm off the rails. My chin dips as I let out a weighty sigh. In the reflection, I see the empty bedroom through the bathroom door. Even from in here, it looks cold and desolate without Jason around. I turn and face the inevitable emptiness.

The towel drops from my hand as I saunter forward, my feet practically dragging across the bathroom's tile floor. I'm too drained to lift my heavy legs. The bedroom's carpeting does a better job of cushioning my steps, but not my feelings. I drag myself to the far side of the bed, where the jewelry box still lies on the floor, open and upside down. I pick it up and turn it around, and my heart sinks, like that feeling you get when you think you've dropped your wallet somewhere in a busy department store. The ring is gone.

My eyes dart to the floor, but I don't see the ring. I drop to my knees, first looking under the bed. When I don't see it, I frantically slide my hands back and forth over the carpet in semi-arc motions, hoping to feel it under my fingers. Nothing.

Shit!

It has to be here somewhere. It didn't just disappear, and it's not that small. What the fuck? What do I do? Jason is going to kill me. He was going to propose. And now, I've lost the ring. But then, it hits me. I remember, the dresser is empty; his clothes are gone. Maybe he changed his mind. He got scared and ran. Why would he have left the ring? No, I can't believe Jason would run away like that. He wouldn't. There must be another explanation. He didn't pack his stuff. Somebody else was here. The apartment door was unlocked. Anybody could have walked in. Somebody tried to make it look like Jason left. He's in trouble. I know he is. I need to contact...

A knock on the door disrupts my thoughts. A twinge of excitement hits me. I sprint into the living room, thinking it might be Jason, and that he's misplaced his keys. When I reach the door, rational thought takes over, and I pause before opening it.

"Who is it?" I ask.

"It's the police," a man's deep voice penetrates through the closed door.

My shoulders drop, releasing built-up tension. I open the door to find a uniformed officer, tall, fit, with broad shoulders. He's older, the gray hair showing from under his cap. His face is somewhat familiar, but I can't place it.

"Do you mind if I come in?" he asks. "I'm following up."

I step aside. "Did you find Jason?"

He slowly scans the apartment, pausing on the empty walls where I swear photos used to be, but I can't be certain.

"Can you tell me again when you last saw him?" he questions.

"Yesterday," I quickly answer. "No, wait. It was Sunday."

"Which was it, miss?"

"It was Sunday," I belt out. "I dreamt about him yesterday. I mean this morning. Early morning."

The officer looks at me dubiously.

"I'm sorry," I offer. "I've been getting confused lately with everything that's been happening."

His eyes narrow. "I understand. You said he left a note?"

"No, he didn't leave a note," I answer. "We *received* a note from somebody. It sounds threatening to me."

"May I see it?"

"Yes, of course."

I rush to the table to retrieve the paper, but when I look at it, it's not the note. It's the list of grocery items instead.

Milk, eggs, coffee, bread.

How can that be? I reach into my front pocket for the crumpled paper, but it's not there. Of course not. It's on the table in front of me.

"Is that the note there?" he asks, my back still facing him.

"No. That's just a grocery list. I-I don't know where the note is. I swear it was right here. I'm not making this up."

"Marney," the officer says quietly. I find it strange that he used my first name. "It's me. Everything will be all right."

My eyes rise from the table. It just dawned on me where I've seen the officer before. He was in Mansfield's Market earlier today. He waved at me. I swing my body around to question him, but the officer is gone. The door stands open, and I'm peering down an empty hallway.

Chapter 27

I stare out the window at the parking lot below, its spaces slowly filling from the first shift workers returning home. None of them are Jason. I've been alone for hours now, days, and I don't know what to do or how to handle any of this. I called the police station earlier to ask about the officer who showed up here, but the man who answered said nobody had been sent to my address. He asked if I was safe. I said yes, though I couldn't be sure.

So much has happened; so much I'm confused about. The bruises and wounds, the daydreams or hallucinations, or whatever they are. I can't deal with all that and Jason's disappearance, too. I can't think straight. Where did he go? What's happened to him? The pictures, the ring...what does it all mean? I searched the bedroom for that ring for over an hour and came up empty-handed. How could it have vanished like that? Everything has gone to shit. I'm everywhere at once and nowhere at all.

I pound my fist against the window trim and lean forward, pressing my forehead against the glass. The coolness feels refreshing. I continue staring out until I see more of myself in the glass than I do the vehicles down below. I turn away from the window and look toward the kitchen. I can almost see Jason gliding effortlessly between the sink and the stove, the stove and the refrigerator, preparing dinner for us. I smile. And then his image fades away, as does my smile, and I'm alone again. Alone, worried, and hungry.

I don't remember eating anything today. I can't keep this up. It's not healthy for the baby or me. But I can't eat without feeling sick, and I don't have the energy to make anything, even if I could keep it down. I'm so tired. I need to lie down and rest my eyes. That's all. Then I'll figure out something to eat.

I amble my way to the couch and collapse onto the cushions. They've never felt so comfortable. I look at the ceiling and watch the popcorn white slowly dim to a grayish color before finally turning black. Everything is quiet. Even the dripping faucet is cooperating tonight and sparing me its grating rhythmic beats. I force myself not to be afraid of sleeping. All I need is a few minutes. Just a few min...

The brilliant light through my eyelids catches me off guard before the cold hits me. I put my hand in front of my eyes to keep from going blind while I squint ever-so-slightly to let my vision acclimate to my surroundings. The chilled air bathes my skin, causing goosebumps to form up and down my arms. My feet are so cold, like I'm standing on blocks of ice. I look down to find I'm half right. I'm standing, but not on ice. I'm barefoot, on cold, hard, white tile squares. I'm wearing a white gown. Not the kind you wear to a dance, but one they give you before going in for surgery. A strong smell of antiseptic drifts across my nostrils, and I wrinkle my nose in discontent. I lift my eyes to ascertain where I am. The three walls in front of me are tiled, like the floor, only with smaller rectangular pieces. There are stainless steel countertops along two of them, and white cabinetry along the third, their glass doors displaying colorful bottles of some sort within. Also along that wall, beside the last cabinet, there is a white door with a small opaque window. Everything is so white and clean. Where the fuck am I?

I feel my gown begin to flow and dance across my skin, and I realize the cold air is blowing at my back. I step forward and glance behind me, then stagger backward at the sight. The entire wall, from left to right, has two rows of tiny, stainless steel doors along its face, like what you'd expect to see at the morgue. My heart knocks against the inside of my chest. Holy fuck! Is that where I am?

Am I at the morgue? What the hell am I doing here? How did I get here? I begin to turn toward the door when I bump into a wheeled table, almost tipping it over. I jump away, startled. I realize what's on the table when an arm falls out from under a white sheet, exposed from my clumsy disturbance. My chest feels like it's caving in, and I struggle to catch my breath.

Oh my God! Oh my God! Oh my God! What do I do?

My lips stay sealed, though all I want to do is scream. I shuffle sideways past the table, avoiding the arm for fear it might come alive and grab me. I'd watched too many horror movies when I was younger to want to tempt fate. I'm just about to reach the door when I hear a voice. It's not coming from inside the room, but rather, from inside my head.

He's not coming back.

Fuck, Toby. Why did you have to put that in my head? I slowly turn to look over my shoulder, the dead body taunting me to come back. I swallow. Do I really want to do this? I have to. I need to know. My feet pivot on the cold, hard tiles, the chilled air crawling up under the flowing cotton linen, stinging my bare legs. I step up to the table, surveying the contour of the body under the sheet. It's a man's shape. I breathe in through my mouth, and my body shudders. I grab the end of the sheet near the body's head, squeezing it tightly in my hand, unable to move. I try pushing past the nervousness, but find myself on the verge of hyperventilating instead.

Just yank it like a Band-Aid. Get it over with. You're worrying over nothing. You know it's not him.

Do I, though? If I knew, I wouldn't have turned back. My muscles tense, and my hand begins to quiver like it's fighting my decision. My lungs convulse, forcing air, quick and shallow, in and out of my mouth like I'm taking a Lamaze class. I slam my eyelids shut and bob my head, knowing what's coming. A calmness washes over me, my breathing slows, and I open my eyes, ready and confident. I pull the sheet down and...

My upper body shoots up, gasping for air, like that feeling you've been underwater too long, lungs burning, but you thankfully make it to the surface just before you drown. Daylight shines through the living room window. I slept through the night. What the hell did I wake from, anyway? That dream was...

"Are you all right, Marn?"

His voice is unmistakable. I swing my legs off the couch and sit upright, thinking I must still be dreaming. I sit and listen. No dripping. No thumping. No leaves crunching. Only silence. Until... there isn't.

"Did you hear me out there?" his voice echoes from the bedroom. "You gotta start getting ready if we're going to make it before dark."

The air around me closes in and offers a soothing hug. It's Jason! He's back!

Chapter 28

I practically trip over my feet as I sprint to the bedroom. Jason came back while I was asleep. I've lost track of how long he was gone. I knew he wouldn't leave me. I knew he couldn't desert his baby. He's such a wonderful man. But why didn't he wake me? Was I that far gone that I didn't hear him come in?

I charge into the bedroom full-steam. Jason's back is to me while he stuffs some balled-up socks into a duffel bag. He doesn't have a chance to react before I slam into him, wrapping my arms around him from behind. The force from my excited bear hug knocks him off balance, and he stumbles forward, catching himself on the mattress with a stiff arm.

"Hey! Ow! What the hell?" he snaps.

His harsh tone surprises me, and I quickly release him and step back, thinking I may have hurt him.

"Oh my God!" I reply. "I'm sorry. Did I hurt you?"

He turns with a grin on his face. "No, you just surprised me. What was that about?"

"I'm just happy to see you," I answer. "I was getting worried. Where were you? Why didn't you call me?"

He gives me a perplexed look.

"What are you talking about? I've been here all morning."

"No, you haven't," I argue. "You've been gone for...I don't know, two days."

"What? Have you forgotten to take your meds again?"

"My meds? What? No! I'm being serious. You left to take care of something and didn't come back for two days. I was worried sick. I even went to the police earlier today. I mean, yesterday."

"The police? Were you dreaming again?"

"That's not funny, Jason. It's been really rough here without you. Strange things have been happening. People are acting weird. I thought I lost you."

"Okay, okay," Jason returns, grabbing my forearm and pulling me into an embrace. "It's okay. I'm here. Shhhhh."

He squeezes me tightly. I feel his warm breath on the top of my head.

"The police wouldn't take me seriously," I add.

"I still don't know what you mean," he says. I feel his grip on me loosen. It's slight, but I notice. "What do you mean you went to the police yesterday?"

"As I said, when you didn't come home, I went to the police to file a missing person's report."

Jason pulls away from me, maintaining contact by sliding his hands down my arms to my wrists. I wonder why he doesn't question me about them being torn up.

"Marney, we were together all day yesterday. Don't you remember? I drove you to pick up your car at the automotive center."

"The automotive center?"

"Yeah. You got an oil change. We agreed we didn't want to take my truck on the long trip."

"Trip?" I question. "I don't know..." I stumble with my thoughts, looking down at the carpet as if I'll find some answers there. While my eyes flutter back and forth, they catch sight of my wrists, and I realize why Jason hasn't mentioned anything. There's nothing wrong with them. No marks. No scarring. I shake my head and try to recover my words. "What trip? I don't remember anything about a trip."

"What? We discussed this," Jason says, releasing my wrists. "We even talked last night about possibly staying longer than the week."

"I-I don't remember any of this," I tell him while rubbing my forehead, trying to draw the memories forth. "Where are we going?"

"You're kidding, right? You said you'd never been to Vermont, so…"

"Vermont?" I question animatedly. My thoughts immediately snap to the picture of the two of us on that ridge, both wearing Vermont hats.

"Don't tell me you're having second thoughts?" he questions, showing his disappointment. "Marney, you can't keep doing this. It's not healthy for you to stay cooped up in this apartment all the time. You've gotta stop blaming yourself for what happened. It wasn't your fault. Christ, do we have to keep doing this over and over again?"

"No, no," I jump in, confused about the whole situation, but I see how much it's upsetting Jason, and I can't lose him again. "I just forgot about it," I continue. "That's all. I haven't been sleeping well, and my brain is a little foggy. I haven't changed my mind. If we made plans to go to Vermont, then I want to go."

"Are you sure?" Jason asks.

I bite my lower lip and nod. "Yeah. Let's go."

"It'll be fun," Jason assures me. "I promise. Besides, the leaves are beautiful this time of year."

A memory hits me. The neighbor. She said that exact thing. *The leaves are beautiful this time of year.*

Jason rubs his hand up and down my left arm and flashes me that dimpled smile that I can't resist. I smile back.

"Now, come on," he says. "You've gotta start packing. We don't want to leave too late." Then, he dashes to the closet and retrieves something from the floor. He swings around excitedly to show me what he's holding. "Oh, and look...matching duffel bags. I got you one too. His and hers." He throws it on the bed beside his, and I tense up. It's the same duffel bag that I found earlier - the one with the pictures and the ring, only it looks much newer. My awkward gaze catches his attention.

"What?" he asks. "What's the matter?"

"Th-the bag."

"What about it?"

"It looks..."

I go silent, looking at Jason's expression. I can tell he thinks I'm losing it. I am. But he can't know that. Not after I've only just gotten him back.

"It looks great!" I tell him, faking a smile. "This is all going to be great."

"Okay, then. Get a move on." He nudges the duffel closer to me.

I roll up a few pants and shirts and stuff them inside the bag, inspecting the interior lining as I do, as if a certain ring box might suddenly appear. It's a foolish thought, but it nags at me with every article I pack.

After a short while, when all of our clothes and personal hygiene products are safely tucked away, we scoop up the bags and are ready to hit the road. I lead the way to the apartment door when Jason tells me he forgot something in the bedroom. My thoughts click to the box with the engagement ring. Is that it? Is he trying to be sneaky? Is he going to propose to me in Vermont? My heart begins to palpitate faster as my nerves kick in. The excitement washes over me, and my palms become tacky with sweat. I try to contain myself, thinking I can't let on that I know anything, and then a knock at the door aids in distracting me. The thought is wiped clean from my brain as I ponder who it could be. I open the door to find Mrs. Blumgard looking at me peculiarly. Her eyes shift to my hand holding the duffel bag, and she curls her lip unabashedly. I open my mouth to speak, but she cuts me off before I can get a word out.

"Going somewhere?"

Her tone bites into me, though it shouldn't. I've had enough dealings with her that it should roll off my shoulders. It doesn't.

"Hi, Mrs. Blumgard," I say as politely as possible while trying not to bite the tip of my tongue off. "Yes. All packed for a trip to Vermont."

"Vermont, huh?"

"That's right." I give her a side-eyed glare as if to say *what business is it of yours*.

"That's an adventurous thing to be going off on a trip like that by yourself."

I shake my head at the woman. "Oh, no. Not by myself. Jason and I are both going." I turn sideways to let her have a peek into the apartment as I point behind me into the bedroom. Her face scrunches, and she leans in slightly, squinting her eyes as if she's trying to read an eye chart. I find it somewhat amusing until I turn my head to look for myself and find the bedroom light off and the apartment dead silent.

"What's that, now?" Mrs. Blumgard screeches. "What are you trying to show me? Who's there?"

I gulp as the weight of the bag in my hand feels like it's pulling me through the floor. I press my hip to the door, slowly closing it on Mrs. Blumgard as I mumble, "I've got to go." I turn fully to face the apartment, my eyes scanning the quiet emptiness. A sudden bout of loneliness takes hold, and I shiver. My arms and legs go numb.

"Jason?" I call out.

I already know the vacant room's response. Jason's not there. He never was.

The old, ragged duffel drops from my hand.

Chapter 29

I don't even notice my hand trembling until I bite down on the skin of my finger, my teeth having whittled the overhanging portion of my nail to nonexistence. It stings for a second, but I distract myself by moving on to the next finger beside it.

My eyes burn. The tears I've wept have long dried, leaving streaks of sticky patches down my cheeks. The floor moves in and out of focus as my upper body rocks back and forth, my butt clinging to the edge of the lounge chair. What is happening to me? Why do I keep having strange visions - people and things appearing and then disappearing? Jason is here one moment, and then gone the next. Vanished. One minute, I'm held captive or running away from somewhere, someone, and then I'm suddenly back to my reality, where everything is normal. Well, not exactly normal, but I'm safe. Fuck, I don't even know what's real anymore.

I pull my fingers from my lips and look at my hands and wrists. There isn't a mark on them. No gash across my palm where I'd cut myself. No burns along my wrists where the rope that had bound me dug into my skin while I struggled to free myself. But I saw it. I felt it. I was there in someone's living room, tied and held captive on a dingy, smelly couch. Even after I had returned from wherever my mind had taken me, the scars of those experiences, both emotional and physical, remained.

I think.

No, I know it; they were there. The skin still itches where the scars should be, only they, too, have disappeared like everything else around me.

I shimmy in the chair a bit, and the front legs scrape against the hardwood, sending a chill down my spine. I don't know how I came to be here or why I chose this seat. I hate this chair. Something about it disturbs me, but Jason wanted to keep it, and Toby seems to like it. If I knew which apartment he lived in, I'd drop it off outside his door. If he even lives in this building.

I don't know what to do. I want Jason back. I don't know where he ran off, but I need him here. I want him to call me, to hear his voice. I need to know that he's all right. I need him to tell me that *I'm* all right. My lower lip quivers with fear, and I bite down on it to keep it still. It feels numb, like nothing is there, so I dig my teeth in deeper. My jaw clenches tighter, searching for some sensation. Anything.

I clasp down harder, tighter, until my front tooth pierces the meaty part of my lip, and blood dribbles down my chin. I wince, finally feeling what I longed for. I swipe my hand across my chin to remove the blood, then look at my red-stained fingers. I reach back up with my index finger to touch the slice in my lip and reel from the instant sting. I let my tongue dance across my lip to clean the wound as I push myself up from the chair to visit the bathroom mirror and inspect the damage.

The light is dimmer than usual - more golden than it should be. It's the kind of light that makes everything look like an old photograph. I stare at myself in the mirror, my eyes bloodshot and devoid of the life they used to carry. My cheeks are no longer pale, replaced with a blushy red, like a baby's bottom after having sat in a wet diaper too long. I roll my lip down with my finger to see the extent of the gash my tooth has caused. The cut is vertical down my entire lower lip, and swollen at each side of the opening. It doesn't look like a bite mark, which I would have expected to be a horizontal slice. I rub my tongue over it several times, enduring the painful tingling. It's deep. I still taste blood with every swipe.

Using my thumb and index finger, I pull at the flaps of skin under my eyes to widen them, looking for the ends, or perhaps, the beginnings, of the creeping streaks of red shooting in all directions. The wall sconces flicker and illuminate brighter. The bathroom lights up, and my pupils constrict from the glow. I release the skin at my upper cheek and blink a few times to let the tear ducts re-moisturize the lenses before gently closing my eyes to quell the burning. When I reopen them, the lighting is back to the musty, yellowish hue. I reach up and tap on the left sconce, but with no change. I shake my head and huff in dissatisfaction. My apartment, my life, my entire world is going to shit, and no amount of subtle taps can fix that amount of broken.

I give a final swipe of my tongue to soothe the ache in my lip, then turn to leave the bathroom. When my eyes meet the exit, my body stiffens, and my shoulders jump up to meet my ears. The beginnings of a scream form in the back of my throat, but it never makes its way out of my mouth before the fist of the man standing in the doorway meets my face.

The cracking sound invades my ears, like two billiard balls colliding. My head jerks back, and my body stumbles backward. I slam into the tile wall, and my feet slip out from under me. I slide down the slick surface, landing hard on my ass. My eyes want to close, but I force myself to stay conscious, alert. Blood pools in my mouth, some of it trickling out of the corners and onto my shirt. I tip my head down and spit a painting of blood onto the floor. A line of red spittle clings for dear life to my lip before the force of my mouth closing causes it to break and spill off my chin. I snap my eyes up to look at my attacker, but as with everything else, there is nobody there. Panicked, my body jittery, I shove myself from the wall and swing my head from side to side, fearing the man might have somehow gotten behind me. I kick my leg up and forward aggressively, like a cornered wild beast, thinking there might still be someone in front of me that I can't see. I hear my own grunts through wheezing breaths, my throat tightening, threatening to cut off my air supply. My eyes dart around the empty bathroom. My ears sharpen, listening for footsteps beyond the tile walls that never break the silence. The man. He's gone. Or was he ever here?

The bitter sting in my lip tells me he was. No, that was from me biting it. Or was it?

Vertical slice, not horizontal.

My eyes drift to the blood on the floor, the red liquid following the white grout lines between the tiles like a flowing stream. This just happened. The blood is still fresh. I touch my lip again, the vengeful sting still present, sharper than before. My tongue glides along the inside of my lower lip. There is a lump there that hadn't been. I look to the door again and scream.

"Get out! Get out of here!"

I hear no movement. I am unsure if I am screaming at the person who hit me, or if I am directing the harsh shrieks to the uncontrollable thoughts in my head.

"Get out of here," I say again, this time in a calmer voice.

I sit on the floor a little longer, letting my breathing settle and my nerves calm. My muscles are so tense, I feel that if I move too quickly, I'll pull one of them. I press my palms to the floor, my right fingers mingling with the crimson liquid, and I slowly heft myself onto my feet. My breathing is still heavy, but slower, more relaxed. The lights flicker and brighten to normalcy. I lean into the vanity, using its surface as a crutch, and turn to the mirror to see the extent of the injury to my face. If not for the hard counter holding me upright, I would have fallen back to the floor. Save for the bloodshot eyes and rosy, salt-laden cheeks, there isn't a blemish on me. My lip is solid. No cut. I feel for the lump with my tongue, but there isn't one. I twist my body and look down at the floor.

Clean.

The gleam from the lights shines against its surface. *What the hell? What is going on? Why is this happening? How is the floor clean of blood? How is my lip healed?*

I look back at my reflection, the image of my shirt, complete with red blotches stained across the front, glaring back at me. I bring my hand to my chest and feel the warm, wet liquid against my skin. I pull my hand away and stare confusedly at the blood. *How?*

"Get out of here." The words exit my mouth as a barely audible whisper.

Chapter 30

Drip.
Drip.
Drip.

I stare out the window into the parking lot even as the kitchen faucet beckons. It's relentless, always dripping. Why is it so loud?

Drip. Drip. Drip.

The wind picks up and howls its discontent. It sweeps across the window with a whistling sound, mixed with a subtle hum, like the sound of street-lights coming to life, only the humming is intermittent. When the wind dies down and the whistling fades, the hum persists. It's strange until I realize the hum isn't emanating from outside the glass but from within the apartment. I turn my head away from the window and spot my vibrating phone on the living room coffee table, the screen lit up. I feel a twinge in my chest, and I recklessly charge like a bull in a china shop to answer it.

I don't recognize the number, but I click the button anyway.

"Hello?" My voice sounds anxious, desperate.

At first, there's nothing, only a brittle hiss, that sound you hear when a radio station goes off the air. Then, from under the static, if I listen hard enough, I hear it. There's a voice whispering my name. It's calm, smooth, as if reading it from a list.

I don't know why, but I whisper back. "Marney?" as if there is another me on the other end of the line. Then, I say louder, "Jason?"

The static cuts out, and the line goes dead.

When I pull the phone away and check the call log, it displays Jason's boss's number. Frantically, I dial the number back. He must know something, or maybe Jason is with him.

The line rings. Again. Then a third time before someone picks up.

"Hello?" the voice comes through the speaker, but it's not Jason's boss. It's a woman's voice.

"Hello," I answer. "Who is this? Is Jason there?"

There's silence for a moment that lasts for an eternity, then the woman speaks.

"Oh, I'm sorry, hun. Haven't you heard?"

"Heard?" I question. "Heard what?"

"It's about your ...." Static rings out. "He's..."

The static kicks back on, burying the voice behind its penetrating buzz.

"What?" I yell. "I can't hear you. Say it again."

The static dissipates long enough for me to hear the words "...found his..." before the call abruptly ends.

"No, no!" I scream out, pressing my thumb several times against the call button, as if I wasn't sure once would be enough.

Someone answers before I even hear the first ring.

"Marney, is that you?"

"Steve, oh my God! Thank goodness. Is Jason..."

The voice cuts me off. "No, Marney, it's me, John."

I hear the name, but I can't put a face to it.

"John?" I question.

"Yes. That's right. Are you okay? Did you need something? I can bring it with me when I swing by later today."

"Later today?" I glance toward the window, the sun's rays now faded, leaving only the darkened night sky. "I'm sorry, who is this?" I ask.

"It's John," the voice says. "You remember me, don't you?"

"John? I'm sorry, I don't..."

"It's okay, Marney. Everything will be all right. You're safe now."

"Safe?"

"Yes. You're safe."

I don't know who the man is on the other end of the line, but his words are soothing. It's a voice I could find myself listening to when I'm restless, to help me fall asleep.

"But...but what about Jason? Is *he* safe?"

The line goes silent, only a sharp exhale, like the person let out a frustrated breath in response to my question.

"I'll see you soon, Marney."

The call ends, and I'm left with only the numbing silence, once again.

Except for the leaky faucet.

Drip. Drip. Drip.

Who was that man? He said his name was John, but I can't think of who that could be. Is it one of Jason's friends? One of his coworkers? And why would he be coming here? *Shit! I'm a mess.* I look down at my shirt, the splotches of dried blood looking like a Rorschach test. I've got to clean myself up.

Before I can move, there's a knock at the door.

Shit! Shit! How can he be here already?

The unspoken answer wouldn't surprise me. I've probably lost two hours without realizing it. I look at my shirt again. The blood is gone. Same shirt, no blood. Not even the hint of a stain. I should have known.

A second knock pulls my attention back. I race to the door, but before I reach for the knob, I press my palms to the smooth wood and listen.

"Who is it?" I ask.

No answer. My shoulders tense.

"Who is it?" I raise my voice to just under a yell.

"It's Toby."

My shoulders relax, and I softly exhale my relief.

I open the door to find Toby staring up at me with those same expressionless eyes. His hands are tucked into the open sides of his denim overalls like pockets. The toes of his bare feet scrunch against the hallway's carpeting like he's anxious.

"I don't know if you should be here right now, Toby," I tell him. "It's getting late."

His eyes shift into the apartment. "He's not here."

I flinch at the boy's remark. "What?"

He directs his eyes to my stomach and holds them there for a few seconds, making me feel uncomfortable, before he raises them back to mine. I instinctively bring my hand to my belly.

"Um, no," I reply. "Jason isn't here."

I say the words like it's nothing, as if they don't cause every inch of my stomach to knot up, when all I want to do is crumble to the floor in a heap. I still may, but Toby doesn't need to be a witness to it.

"Not Jason," Toby replies, barging into the apartment as he always does and hopping into his favored chair. "John."

I feel a tingle that starts at my ear and shoots down the side of my neck before burrowing under my shoulder blade. Before closing the door, my eyes catch sight of the neighbor's yellow door. *Wasn't it green?*

I swing the door closed just as Toby begins his ritual leg kicking.

Thump.

Thump.

Thump.

I turn and give him an inquisitive look as I make my way to the couch on his right.

"Why did you mention John not being here?" I question. "Do you know John?"

The boy remains silent, letting his heels do the talking.

Thump. Thump. Thump.

His eyes are fixed straight ahead into the kitchen, paying no attention to me, as if I'm not even present.

"Toby, I asked you a question. How do you know John? When did you talk to him?"

Toby's eyes don't waver. He doesn't answer. He acts like he didn't hear the question. Still, his little feet swing back and forth against the front of the chair, the sound matching the beat of my heart.

Thump. Thump. Thump.

My jaw clenches. I react out of character, slapping my palm against the couch cushion beside me. I yell in frustration.

"How the fuck do you know John, Toby?"

The boy's legs immediately halt their swinging. His head swivels slowly in my direction. His eyes stare vacantly at me. No, *through* me.

"I don't," he answers.

He slides off the chair and begins calmly walking toward the door. As he passes by me, I grab his wrist, slightly annoyed by his childish games.

"How did you know about John?" I ask again, my tone more even.

Toby looks down at my hand around his wrist, then veers his glance to my eyes.

"It's okay, Marney," he whispers. "It wasn't your fault."

I shake my head, confused. "What did you..?"

I feel his arm twist in my grip as he turns his hand up. I look down as his fingers loosen from a fist. I narrow my gaze. In his palm lie my keys, the pewter cow gazing at me. I grab the keys and release the boy's wrist. I get lost in my thoughts for a moment. I stare at the cow, even as I hear the apartment door open, the word balloon from the bovine's mouth displaying a new phrase. "Love, Laugh, Farm-ily."

Then, I hear Toby's voice. "You're safe now."

I look up from my stupor. The apartment door is open, the boy gone.

The words echo in my ear, the same as what the mysterious person on the phone said to me. *You're safe now.*

Chapter 31

I need air. It's like I can't breathe. The walls are closing in on me, compressing the oxygen from my lungs, suffocating me. The ceiling light is too bright, causing the shadows to pulse like they're breathing. I squeeze my fingers tighter, clutching the keys in my hand. I need to get out.

Without grabbing my jacket, which hangs on a peg by the door, I burst from the apartment, gasping for openness. In my haste to leave, I collide with a man outside in the hall. He brushes back.

"Oh my gosh," I say. "I'm so sorry."

"It's all right," he replies. "No harm done. You're in quite a hurry."

The man is middle-aged, maybe fifty or fifty-five. He's short and bald with dark-rimmed glasses. He's not fat, but he's showing the beginnings of a beer belly. I look down at my own stomach and notice a slightly similar bulge. *That can't be*, I think.

Then the man speaks up again. "You're not hurt, are you?"

"Oh, ah, no."

The man doesn't attempt to move, only smiles and nods.

"Are you John?" I question.

The man turns his head sideways, looking at me through the corner of his eyes like he's confused.

"No. Peter," he answers. "Apartment 3C." He points to the next door down the hall on my side.

"Oh, Mrs. Blumgard's apartment," I blurt. "Are you her son?"

"No, I'm...wait. Who?" He shakes his head like he's shaking away cobwebs.

"Mrs. Blumgard," I repeat. "That's her apartment."

"I'm sorry, ma'am, but you're mistaken."

Ma'am again?

"I don't know who the woman is you're referring to, but *I'm* the tenant in apartment 3C. Have been for two years now."

"No," I say, shaking my head in disbelief. "That's not right. Mrs. Blumgard lives there. I've been her neighbor for about eight years. We just spoke earlier today."

"Ooookay," the man dribbles off, rolling his eyes at me. "I've gotta go."

He squeezes past me, pulling keys from his pocket. As he slides one into the doorknob's key slot, he glances over at me. When he sees me still staring in his direction, he quickly averts his eyes back to the knob before opening the door and vanishing into the apartment. I don't get it. How could he not know Mrs. Blumgard? That *is* her apartment. That guy must be messing with me. It's not like she just suddenly disappeared. I can't deal with this right now.

I scramble down the hall to the staircase, remembering my tightening chest and burning lungs. The stale air in this building is too much to take. Down two flights, I exit the rear entrance into the parking lot. The night is cool and dark. If not for the illuminated lamppost, it would be pitch black.

I turn my face to the sky, close my eyes, and inhale as deeply as possible. A slight breeze washes over me, but I don't notice the chill. I take it all in, letting the quiet evening still my troubled thoughts. Toby's words tickle my ears. *You're safe now.* Safe? From what? From who? Then I hear the clinking of metal against metal near the corner of the building, and my eyes snap open. Mr. Jeffries is puffing on a cigarette, his thumb flipping the lid of his Zippo lighter open, and then snapping it shut. Open. Close. Open. Close. He sees me and smiles, the cigarette dangling from his lips.

Open. Close.

I shoot him an unsavory glare. He removes the cigarette from his mouth, spits at his feet, then takes another puff before slipping the lighter into his shirt pocket. He gives me a flip of his hand as a wave, and then disappears around the corner.

Fuck! Creepy-ass perv.

I bend over, supporting myself with my hands pressed to my knees. Breathe. Breathe. I close my eyes and rub my forehead, relieving the stress. Then, his voice hits me like a fist to a punching bag.

"There you are."

It's an innocent enough comment, but something about the voice sets my skin crawling. I don't look to see who it's coming from. Instead, I turn to run, but am met by a cold, hard slab of concrete that almost shatters my nose. Suddenly, the air feels different. Thick. No breeze. I turn back, and the parking lot is gone, replaced with four gray walls, dust particles fluttering about the dimly lit space.

"No, no, no," I whisper. I look down to see the metal shackle clasped around my ankle. I'm back. I don't know how, but I'm back in someone's basement. Trapped. Alone.

My pulse quickens.

"What the fuck?" I mumble, grabbing for the chain that's snaked along the concrete floor. "How is this possible? How am I here? I wasn't here. I was outside. I got out."

My body stiffens. Why did I say that? *I got out.* I meant, I *was* out. I was home. Outside that awful apartment. Where it happened. I don't want to think about that. I can't. I need to focus on…

The door at the top of the staircase swings open. Light invades the stairwell. My back presses harder against the concrete wall as a foot steps through the open door onto the first tread.

"Who's there?" I yell, wrapping the chain around my fist like brass knuckles.

The door slams closed.

"Show yourself, you mother fucker!"

I hear the boots descending the stairs.

Thump.

Thump.

Thump.

"What do you want with me?" I scream, holding back tears. I have no time for them. I know how this plays out. I've been here before.

A figure comes into view, draped in shadow. This is where it ends. I ready myself, knowing I will snap from this nightmare and be back in the parking lot, back to where I'll be safe again.

You're safe now.

The words permeate through the walls, along with a fervent smell of antiseptic that stings my nostrils. Something isn't right. I haven't woken. I'm still in the basement. That's when I realize it. This nightmare isn't over.

Chapter 32

Dust lands on my lips faster than I can lick it away. The smell of antiseptic drifts off to where it came from, replaced with the pungent stench of stale air and mildew. My heart pounds its dread as a bead of sweat slinks from my temple down my cheek. I shouldn't be here; this was supposed to end. I close my eyes and tap my foot on the hard floor, no doubt kicking up more dust. None of it matters. I know when I reopen them, I'll be back outside, rubbing away goosebumps from my arms. It's all a dream. A horrible nightmare that I'm ready to wake from. With that promising thought, I force my eyes open, but my surroundings remain unchanged. I shouldn't be here.

But I am.

In the encompassing darkness, a man stands before me at the bottom of the stairs. My eyes strain, peering into the only light cast in this damp, dark hell, but they still can't penetrate the shadow obscuring my captor's face. I hear his heavy breaths, and I tremble.

"Hey there, kitty," the man begins. "I brought you a treat." He squats and places a round, yellow dish on the floor, then slides it toward me like he's playing shuffleboard. It clinks off a section of chain and comes to a stop near my right foot. "Eat."

"Fuck you!" I say through clenched teeth.

"Don't you worry your pretty little head," the man replies. "We'll get to that part soon enough."

My stomach gurgles.

"Now eat, I said."

"And I said, Fuck you!" I kick the dish back at him. It tips, spilling its contents out onto the floor.

"You stupid, ungrateful, little bitch."

The man storms forward. I brace myself, pulling the chain taut, ready to use it. I've never been in a physical altercation before, but that won't stop me from beating the shit out of this guy. When he is almost upon me, I swing my arm with everything I've got. Unfortunately, my lack of fighting experience shines through, and my fist lands with a thud on his upper arm.

"You fucking cow!" the man shouts.

My keychain flashes in my head. *I hate cows.*

"That hurt." He swings his leg and kicks me in the gut. My body folds in half, my knees give way. I drop to the concrete, gasping for air. I can't breathe. My arms blanket my stomach as I try to force a cough, anything to convince my lungs to intake some oxygen.

A hand latches onto my hair and shoves my head forward and down. I land on the floor, curling into a fetal position, wondering if this is how I die. I make a wheezing sound, which comforts me. It lets me know air is getting through. The comfort doesn't last long. Fingers tangle into my hair as the shadowy figure clasps tightly and yanks me forward. I force myself back to my knees to prevent him from tearing the clump out by the roots.

"You think you can disrespect me?" he yells, dragging me across the floor.

I try to scream, either from pain or from fear, but the sound eludes me while my diaphragm still struggles to recover from the initial blow. My hands scrape across the basement floor as I try to keep up with his pace. He stops and muscles my face to the floor. I'm able to turn my head enough so my cheek flattens to the cold surface instead of my nose. Something sharp, a rock maybe, digs into my cheek as he applies more weight. Spit trickles from my mouth as my breathing begins to restore.

"When I tell you to eat, you eat."

The man's hand slides my face forward toward the mound of slop that had fallen from the bowl. I feel my cheek burn as granules of dirt scrape across the skin.

"Now eat!" The man demands, applying more pressure to my head.

The clump of food is inches from my mouth. The smell hits me, and I realize it's cat food. Before I have a chance to react to the unsavory slop, the fucker snatches my right arm and twists it behind my back, almost dislocating it. Yanking my hair, he pulls me back onto my knees and thrusts my face forward over the cat food until my lips feel the wetness.

"Don't make me snap this twig from your body," he seethes, pulling my arm almost past its breaking point. My shoulder screams in agony. "Do it now, you filthy whore."

My tongue flicks out, touching the tip of the moist splatter. My tastebuds flare their dissatisfaction, and my face scrunches.

"That's it," the man says. "Eat it up." He shoves my face down more.

My lips open and suck in the cat food. I force it down the back of my throat, hoping to bypass my tongue so the taste doesn't cause me to throw up. When the pile is gone, the man holds me firm, my warm breath bouncing off the liquid stain and back into my face.

"Now lick the floor clean," he says.

"*You* lick it, you son of a bitch," I manage to squeak out through labored breathing.

The man pulls on my hair, yanking my head back. He releases my arm, which drops to the floor after a sharp pain shoots through my shoulder. Then, with his free hand, he punches me in the side of my face. I feel something small crash into the inside of my opposite cheek, and I know it was a portion of tooth. The taste of my blood's iron washes over my tongue. My body shivers under his grip. My eyes dart up to meet my abuser, but I see only shadow, like my mind can't process his appearance.

"I've been nice to you so far," he says. "Do you really want to anger me?"

My lips quiver.

"I asked you a question," he barks. "Do you want to upset me?"

"N-no," I whisper. My mind tries to offer comfort by telling me this isn't real. I want to believe it, but no matter how hard I try, I can't convince myself. The feel, the smell, the taste, it's all too much to pretend it's not.

"Good girl. Now lick it up." He shoves my face back to the dirty floor, the juices from the disgusting cat food mingling with dust and grime.

My tongue lashes out, slapping against the concrete. I slather it around, lapping up the liquid, the debris, and anything else it touches if it will get this guy away from me.

When I'm finished mopping the floor, the man tugs my hair and grabs onto my shoulder, digging his fingers into my skin through my shirt.

"That's a good kitty. Now, about that 'fuck you' part." He shoves me backward. My ass hits the floor, followed by my elbows. My left arm goes numb as my funny bone cracks against the concrete. My heart is banging against the inside of my ribs like a jackhammer as he unbuttons his jeans. I crawl backward on my butt, digging my heels into the floor and pushing back. He takes a step forward, then stops.

"Jesus Christ!" he belts out, pointing between my legs, where a growing patch of wetness extends from my groin and down my left leg. "You're pissing yourself." He quickly rebuttons his pants. "Disgusting bitch. Now we gotta get you cleaned up."

We? He said we. More than one?

He reaches behind his back and pulls a rag from his back pocket. Then, from his front pocket, he pulls a little brown glass bottle.

I continue to inch my way backward until I hit the wall, the eyebolt holding the chain presses into my back. I stare at the man from a distance, his upper body doused in shadow. I watch him pour some liquid onto the cloth before closing up the bottle and wedging it back into his pocket. Though I can't see it, I can feel his menacing smile as he takes a step forward.

"Stay away from me!" I scream. "Do you hear me? Stay the fuck away from me!"

I hear his taunts as he lurches closer. "Here, kitty, kitty. Be a good little pussy and take your medicine."

When he gets within reach, I flail my arms and legs wildly, hoping something, anything will connect with enough force. He slaps my arms down and slams his palm into my forehead, sending my head smashing into the concrete wall. My vision blurs for a moment, and I feel liquid drip down the back of my neck.

Drip.

Drip.

Drip.

His next words come to me sluggish and drawn out, distorted like a vinyl record playing on slow speed.

"Nighty-night."

I'm helpless as the man's palm compresses against my face, the saturated cloth smothering my nose and mouth. I feel myself fading. Fading. Fad…

Chapter 33

"Everything will be all right." The voice is quiet, barely registering, like someone speaking with cotton in their mouth. "You're safe now."

"Safe?" I mumble my reply.

"That's right; I've got you."

Then, the volume cranks up to ten.

"Run, Marney! Run!"

The leaves are wet under my feet, slick. I can't get good traction. He's right behind me. I won't make it. I won't...

"Hey," a whisper floats over my shoulder. "How's our little angel?"

"Beautiful and asleep," I answer.

"Marney, it wasn't your fault."

"What?"

"I said...Run, Marney! Run!"

I want to, but it feels like I'm running in molasses. I'll never get away. The leaves are too heavy, too slippery. The leaves...

"The leaves are beautiful this time of year."

They are, but I've grown to hate the outdoors. The smell is rancid, like death. The awful stench of...

Antiseptic.

"It's me, John."

"Who?"

"Here, kitty, kitty."

"Run, Marney! Run!"

"I've got you. You're safe now."

"Safe?"

"It's me, John."

"Who?"

Thump.

What was that? Can I hear it again?

Thump.

No, no, no, no, no.

"It wasn't your fault."

"I love you," he says, flashing his dimples.

"I love you too," I reply.

"I've got a surprise for you."

"You do?"

He doesn't answer. He can't. He sees the look on my face. I can't just leave him.

"Run, Marney! Run!"

I can't. My hand burns. I turn my palm up and blood spills to the cold, wet ground.

"The leaves are beautiful this time of year."

The gash in my hand is deep; it won't stop bleeding. What's it from? I don't remember. Don't think about it. Just run.

I can't just leave him.

Just run!

I can't stop shaking. Close your eyes. Close your eyes!

"Here, kitty, kitty."

What did the news reports say? No, no, no, no.

Thump. Thump. Thump.

"How's our little angel?"

"Beautiful."

"It wasn't your fault."

"What?"

I hear the crunching of the leaves.

"Did you think we wouldn't find you?"

The hammer clicks.

"You're safe now."

Click.

"Safe?"

Bang!

My eyes flutter open. I'm sitting upright on the couch, my jaw a little sore. I blink my eyes a few times to adjust to my surroundings. I'm in my apartment. It's bright. Too bright. Sunlight shines in through the window. It's morning. Was I...asleep? How was I asleep so long? It feels like I just sat down.

I twist my head to the left and scream when I see Toby sitting in his favorite chair, his eyes fixed on me.

"Toby!" I say, catching my breath. "Shit! I mean...uh..." Too late to cover it up. Redirect.

"What are you doing here? How did you get in? Wasn't the door locked?"

He doesn't answer but points at the coffee table in front of me. "Can I have one?"

There are three empty Jell-O cups on the table: red, green, and blue. The red one is tipped on its side, a spoon lying next to it.

"Y-yeah," I answer, standing and clearing the table of the used plastic cups. "I think I have more."

I step into the kitchen and dispose of the snack cups. My palm itches as I reach for the refrigerator door, the kind of itch that lingers after a wound heals. A flash of blood pops into my head, but then vanishes as quickly. I open the fridge, and a waft of antiseptic hits my nose. I turn away for a second, and then it's gone. When I look back, two of the three shelves are full of Jell-O containers.

What the hell? Why do I have so many?

"What color do you want?" I call out from behind the open door. The boy doesn't respond. I pick my head up and peek over the door. "Toby?"

The boy is standing by the window, looking out into the parking lot. My heart drops into my stomach.

"Toby, what are you looking at? Is there something going on out there?"

He turns his head to acknowledge me. "I'm looking for him."

I squint. "Looking for who?"

He doesn't answer but calmly walks back to the chair, where he proceeds to kick his legs back and forth.

Thump. Thump. Thump.

I close the refrigerator door without choosing a snack cup and walk back into the living room.

"Can you please stop making that noise, Toby?" I ask politely. "I don't like that sound."

"Me neither," he replies. His swinging legs come to a stop and dangle freely above the floor.

"You didn't answer my question from before. What are you doing here?"

"Mr. Cartledge asked me to come," he says, being freer with his answers.

"Mr. Cartledge?"

"Uh-huh. He asked me to check on you."

"Who's Mr. Cartledge?"

"You know," the boy answers. "John."

My eyes widen. "John?"

Toby goes silent.

"John...Mr. Cartledge asked you to check on me?"

The boy nods, his deep-set eyes burning into me.

"I thought you said you didn't know John," I remind the boy.

"I don't."

"Toby, stop playing these silly games."

"I'm not."

"Then how did he tell you to check on me? Where is he right now?"

Toby swings his eyes to the door. "He's out there."

I turn and look at the closed door.

"He's out there?" I question. "In the hall?"

"Not in the hall. Out *there*." He bobs his head diagonally like I'm supposed to know where he's talking about. "He's been waiting for you."

"Mr. Cartledge is waiting for me?" I ask. " Can you take me to him?"

The boy shrugs. "If you want."

"Yes, I would like that. Can we go now?" I'm trying not to show my emotions. He's being awfully strange, and it's making me nervous.

Toby's eyes shift down and lock on my pants. I look down to see what has his attention - a large wet spot around my crotch.

Embarrassed, I swing my hand in front of my pants. "Oh my God! I'm so sorry, Toby. I'll be right back."

I run into the bedroom to change, my mind racing. *I wet myself.* While I was sleeping? No, while I was...

There. But where? I don't know, damn it! The memory or dream, whatever, drifts away like ash on a windy day. I wipe my legs down with a washcloth and throw on a fresh pair of underwear and pants. When I return to the living room, Toby is gone, as usual, and the front door is wide open.

I'm alone again.

Chapter 34

The apartment feels larger tonight. Not in a normal way. Almost like someone stretched the walls when I wasn't looking. The air still feels thick, heavy, constricting. No matter how much I try to clean or freshen up the place, it doesn't change. Daylight shines through the window, but when I look at my phone, it displays 9:40 pm. I don't know what to believe. I let the words breathe from my lips as a whisper into the stillness.

"What time is it?"

I never imagined, through the layers of air, I'd receive a hushed response.

"Too late."

The voice is Jason's, only he's not here. I know that now. *He's not coming back.* The sound came from behind the wall, to the left of the television. I stand to investigate, pressing my ear to the wall-paper. I hear Jason's voice again, clearer now.

"Marney, open the door."

I turn my curious stare to the door, wondering if it's possible. Could this be an omen? Is Jason standing out in the hall, waiting for me to let him in? It can't be. It isn't real. And yet, something pulls me from the wall and forces my feet in that direction.

I lean in to the door and listen through the wood, but don't hear anything.

"Jason?" I whisper.

From across the room, near the TV, the wall responds. "Open the door."

I twist the knob and pull the door open to find my neighbor standing there, her hand raised in a fist, like she was about to knock. Only, it's not my new neighbor, but my previous neighbor, Angie.

"Angie!" I say excitedly. "I didn't think I'd see you again."

"What? Why not?" She squeezes her lips at the edges, causing small indents at each end. Her piercing brown eyes narrow to little slits as if confused by my comment.

"Well, because you didn't say goodbye when you moved out."

"What are you talking about, Marney? I haven't moved out."

My eyes drift over her shoulder at a small wreath of fake flowers hanging on the beige door behind her - the same flowers Angie used to hang.

I feel my face go flush.

"Are you okay, Marney?" she asks.

I shift my eyes to hers and fake a smile. "Oh, yeah, I was just playing. You know me, always the jokester." Then comes the uncomfortable silence as we stare at each other, both aware that I'm not being entirely truthful. I relent. "D-did you need something?" I ask.

"Oh, well, I thought I heard Toby over here earlier, and I was wondering if he was still here."

"Y-you know Toby?"

"Of course. Everyone knows Toby."

"Does he live in these apartments?" I question.

"Of course, silly."

"Where? Which unit?"

Just then, Angie's door cracks open, and a little blonde girl timidly peeks out.

"Mommy?"

Angie twists to look at her daughter.

"Just a moment, Sophia. Mommy's talking with her friend."

I smile and wave my fingers at the girl. She eases the door to within an inch of closing until only one eye is showing through the crack.

"Anyway," Angie continues, "I just thought if Toby was still around, maybe I could take him to the park with us. Sophia's been asking for a play-date."

"Oh. N-no," I let out in a surprised stutter. "He ran off some time ago."

Angie displays a small frown. "That's too bad. Sophia was looking forward to it. Another time, then. I'm sure I'll catch up with him one of these days."

"Mommy?" Sophia cries again from behind the door.

"Yes, baby, I'm coming." Angie turns to me with a smile that looks forced. "Well, it was good seeing you, Marney."

"You too," I say, nodding.

She turns and steps back inside her apartment. I close the door and rest my forehead against the hollow panel. Something seems off. Everything about that encounter felt weird, though I have no idea why. And how does she know Toby? *Everyone knows Toby*, she said. *I* don't know Toby. I don't even know which apartment he lives in. But I'm going to find out.

I yank the door open, on a mission, and step into the hall to check with Angie. When I do, I feel my heart drop into my stomach. There is no wreath of flowers on the bright yellow door, only a nickel nameplate with the name "Larson" inscribed upon it.

Completely frustrated, I want to scream and rip my hair out. I only hold back because I know one of my neighbors will call the landlord or the police. I can't handle either one happening. I grit my teeth and go back into my apartment.

Chapter 35

The walls breathe, stealing my oxygen. The clock ticks. The faucet drips. I try to refocus. Every attempt to distract myself with the television is pointless. Every station has been hijacked by news reports...

News reports?

...of death and missing persons. I look away, unable to stomach what they show me. It's all so bad. So horribly bad. I hate it. I don't want to see it.

I think of the neighbor, Angie, asking about Toby. She said she knew him. *Everyone knows Toby.* Mrs. Blumgard also seemed to know him. But now, both Angie and Mrs. Blumgard are gone. And Jason...he's gone, too. Everyone is disappearing from my life. But not Toby. At least he's still with me.

He's still with me.

My eyelids become too heavy to struggle with keeping them open.

He still visits. He's still with me.

My mind calms. I'm so tired. My eyes close.

I feel the wisp of a hand brush against mine, and I jerk my arm back, my eyes sharp and focused. There's nobody beside me. It was all in my head. I feel the tightness in my neck, like a pinched nerve, from nodding off in a seated position. I reach up with my right hand to rub the back of my neck. When I do, something stings into my hand, and I feel liquid drip down under my shirt across my shoulder blade. I pull my hand back, and my eyes fill with panic. There is a deep gash in my hand, from the base of my index finger diagonally to the heel of my palm. Blood pours from the wound, spilling onto my lap and the cushions beside my leg.

"Oh, fuck!" I let out. There's so much blood. And the pain is almost unbearable. I clasp my other hand against the wound to slow the release of blood, gritting my teeth, as every nerve ending in my body fires in contempt. I stand to run to the bathroom to bandage myself, but as I take a step, something catches my feet, and I fall sideways onto the cushions. My head hits the pillow; dust flies into the air. I feel a sneeze coming on, but a nagging buzz in my brain tells me to suppress it, though I don't know why. I force it away. I try to stand again, and that's when I feel the tug on my arms.

The pain in my hand is gone, but I can't move. In front of me, I see an older television on a wheeled cart, and I know exactly where I am. I try to tilt my chin down to assess my predicament, but my head is held down, a strap across it. Voices chime from behind me as a door swings open. I remember this. I close my eyes.

The two men are arguing about some sporting event. One of them turns on the TV and stands in front of me. The other man joins him. I can feel the heat from them. They're close. A boxing match holds their attention. I squint an eye open to see my captors. One of the men is wearing a shirt that looks familiar to me. He's turned just enough where I can almost make out a logo on the breast pocket. He swivels a little more. I can just about make it out. A little more. Just a little more.

Then, something on the television catches my eye. There's a bright red banner at the bottom of the screen with scrolling text. It's a news report update. Something's happened.

"Authorities are still searching for a suspect in the brutal assault of a motorist on Kelley Stand Road who was…"

"Don't look at that," a voice says softly. It's a man's voice.

My eyes shift sideways toward the sound of the words. Someone is sitting in a chair beside the couch. I can't quite make them out; their features are blurry.

"Would you like me to help you sit up?" the man asks.

The realization hits; he's talking to *me*. He knows I'm awake. No sense in pretending any-more.

"I can't move," I tell him. "My arms and legs are tied."

"Are they?" he replies.

My arm twitches at his remark, and I pull it in front of me. I stare at my hand and wrist. No burn marks like last time. The other two men are gone, and I am staring sideways at my bedroom door. I'm back in my apartment. I whisper, "What the fuck?"

"Here, let me help you up," the man says, be-ginning to stand.

"Don't touch me!" I yell.

He sits back down.

"I can sit up on my own."

I push myself upright and sit rigidly, staring at the man. The blurriness fades from my eyes, and I see him clearly now. He is a young man, maybe a year or two younger than me. He's clean-shaven with stubbly, short brown hair, almost like you'd see from someone in the military. He's wearing a green and black plaid button-up shirt that is par-tially hidden behind a bright orange vest, with baggy black cargo pants and black boots. His eyes are a light brown set behind long lashes. His stare is soft and trusting, protective. I feel the tension in my shoulders dissipate.

"Who are you?" I ask. "What are you doing in my apartment?"

"You don't remember me?" he asks.

"I don't know you," I reply confidently.

I watch as his shoulders drop and he lets out a defeated sigh. Then, he looks at me with those gentle eyes and says, "It's me, John."

My heart thumps.

Thump. Thump. Thump.

"John?" I repeat. "John *Cartledge?*"

He smiles. "That's right. You *do* remember."

"N-no. I don't know you. The little boy, Toby, told me about you. You're sitting in his favorite chair. Where is he anyway?"

"Toby couldn't be here today."

"Oh." I feel a headache coming on, and bring my left hand up to rub my temple. "But who are you again?"

"I'm a friend," he answers, his voice calm and soothing. "Come; walk with me."

"What?"

"It will do you some good."

John stands up and offers me his hand in a gentlemanly fashion. I hesitate for a moment, then accept. He eases me to my feet. I expect him to let go after I'm standing, but he continues holding my hand.

"It's this way," he says, escorting me to the door. I follow, his voice making me feel safe.

He opens the door, and we step out into the hall. He urges me forward, but I pause to look at the neighbor's beige door, the wreath of flowers hung below the apartment number 3D.

"You don't have to look at it," John says, gently pulling on my hand.

"I know. But Angie was looking forward to bringing Toby to the park with her daughter. I wish I knew where he ran off to."

"It's okay. It'll all be better after our walk."

We continue down the hall toward the staircase when I hear thunderous footsteps running up from the lower floor. I stop, waiting for what's coming. Two uniformed police officers appear, their demeanor solemn. They walk by us in the direction of my apartment; the second officer, a woman, tips her hat to me. "Excuse me, Miss." The overhead light reflects off her name badge, catching my eye. L. Poole. I know that name.

I stare at their backs, wondering where they are going.

"You don't have to watch," John says, squeezing my hand.

"But I need to know where they are going."

"Marney, it wasn't your fault."

Something torques in my gut, and it's not the baby.

"What?" I question, turning in John's direction, only he's not there. I'm staring down an empty hallway. "Where did..?" My words are cut short as the floor seems to shift and move under my feet.

I swing my hand to the nearest wall to catch my balance. What should be smooth sheetrock feels jagged and rough. I glance down at the carpet, the reds and oranges swirl together, crunching under my feet. Jason's words pop into my head. *The leaves are beautiful this time of year.* I turn my head to my leaning hand, and the wall is not a wall at all, but a large oak tree. The crisp air beats against my skin as I adjust to my surroundings. Then, the pain shoots through my side, and I buckle to the ground, gasping for air. I look at my left side, my shirt soaking up the red liquid like a sponge. My hands shake wildly as I reach for the hem of my shirt. I lift it to see where the blood is coming from. At the sight of the hole, the pain becomes more excruciating. Blood spills out and oozes down my skin like a half-empty bottle of water tipped on its side. I ease the shirt back into place and press my forearm against my side. My other hand aches-not as bad, but enough to get my attention. It, too, is covered in blood, the crimson liquid splashing out onto the leaves beneath me.

I sit frozen, unable to think. I swing my head around, the forest swallowing my sight in every direction. I don't know what to do, where to go. Then I hear a whisper. It's faint. It sounds like John. *Everything is going to be all right.*

I wipe my bloody hand across the front of my chest, staining my shirt. No, not mine. Someone else's. Then I hear Jason's voice. It hits me like a sledgehammer against the back of my skull.

"Run, Marney, Run!"

I shove myself up to my heels, and I run as fast as my feet can carry me. I don't look back. I keep running, not knowing why or where I am going. I continue hearing the words echoing off the trees, slamming into me from all directions.

"Run, Marney! Run!"

So I run faster.

Chapter 36

I kick my legs as fast as they can go, and then kick them harder to go faster, my wounded side punishing me with every step, but I can't stop or slow down. I hold my arm compressed against me as best I can. I don't know which way to go. The leaves crumble and slide under my shoes. I run straight, deeper into the woods where they can't find me.

Who?

I hear the lingering voice in my head.

"Here, kitty, kitty."

It makes me want to vomit. Or is it the morning sickness that has come upon me again? I press my bloody palm to my stomach, hoping to feel a little foot kick. One last kick. Anything. It doesn't come.

I run fifty yards more and have to stop to catch my breath. I lean my shoulder into a tree, my body weakening from loss of blood. I'm growing tired, but I know I must keep going. Ahead of me, I see movement. Someone steps out from behind a tree, and I feel relief. It's a police officer. It's the same older officer who visited me in my apartment, whom I saw in Mansfield's Market that same day. He was staring and waving at me then, just as he is now.

"Help me," I say through labored breaths.

The officer waves me onward. I push off from the tree and stumble forward, my legs wobbly. The leaves crunch with every step. When I get to within a few feet of him, he smiles and extends his arms like he's asking for a hug. I don't have the strength. Instead, I fall forward, collapsing into his out-stretched arms, only, he's not there, and I fall to the ground onto my knees.

I can't keep the tears in any longer, and I break down into a sob. It's not from the pain; my body is already going numb. It's from something else. Fear. Loneliness. My chin drops to my chest in despair, and my eyelids lift. At my knees is a crumpled piece of paper. I recognize it. It must have fallen from my pocket.

I swipe it from the forest floor and begin un-raveling it. Blood from my open wound splatters onto the paper. I smooth out the creases until the page is flat enough for me to see. I thought it was a grocery list, but instead, it is a picture drawn with crayons. A stick-figure woman with brown hair stands beside a house. Next to the woman, holding her hand, is a smaller figure with blonde hair. At the bottom corner, in big shaky letters, I read the words aloud.

"Sophia, age 7."

My eyes burn. When I look up, I'm no longer in the forest but in my apartment. No, not *my* apartment, someone else's. The police are here, too. One of them is the female officer I saw earlier in the hall. Officer Poole.

I glance around the apartment and see a framed picture on the wall. It's the same picture in crayon I picked up off the ground. I'm in Angie's apartment. Why?

I freely walk through the apartment, the police officers moving in slow motion, oblivious to me being here. My eyes keep darting to the drawn picture. There is something off about it, but I can't quite put my finger on it. Poole and the other officer wade by me, weaving in and out of rooms, disturbing items like they're searching for something. Still, my eyes gaze at the picture until a thought pops into my head. It strikes me as odd that Sophia drew her mom with brown hair.

Just then, Officer Poole steps from the bedroom. She's holding a pen in her outstretched arm, and hanging from the end of the pen is a wig of blonde hair. Both officers brush by me like I'm not here and exit the apartment. Through the open doorway, I see them knocking on my door. I open my mouth to tell them I'm over here, but nothing comes out. *How do they not see me?* The knocking persists.

Knock. Knock. Knock.

It's so loud.

Knock. Knock. Knock.

The rapping hurts my eardrums. I cup my hands over my ears to block the sound. It's muffled, but it's still there.

Knock. Knock. Knock.

I want to scream at them, but still, my voice doesn't come. They're ignoring me. Why? I settle for screaming inside my head. I squeeze my eyes shut and frantically shake my head. I don't like the sound of the knocking. It hurts so much.

Then the whispers start.

It only brings pain.

"We found his..."

It only brings pain.

Darkness surrounds me.

It only brings...

Knock, knock, knock.

The knocking at my door disturbs my unsettling thoughts while I gaze out the window to the parking lot below. I stare, and I stare, always searching for something that isn't there.

I turn from the window, saddened and lethargic. The knocking will continue until I answer it. I drag my feet, dreading this part. I know what lies behind door number one. I grab the knob and twist. I know what to expect; it's the same every time. Only, this time, when the door opens, I'm hit with the unexpected.

"Toby?"

He looks at me with those same sullen features I've learned to adopt as my own.

"What are you doing here?" I ask.

"I came to check on you," he answers, parading into my living room like it's become his space.

"Did John send you?" I question, closing the door.

"No."

"Then why would you think you need to check on me?"

Silence floods the air between us for a moment while the boy's stare eats into me.

"Do you remember yet?" he asks.

The leaves are beautiful this time of year.
Run, Marney! Run!
Here, kitty, kitty.
Fucking bitch!
Everything will be all right. You're safe now.
It's me, John.
We found his...

"Remember what?"

Toby's eyes lower to my stomach.

"How's the baby?" he asks.

I stiffen. The boy's comment hits me from out of the blue. It's something I don't expect from an eight-year-old.

"The baby?" I question, placing my palm on my belly. "H-how did you know I was pregnant?"

"I just know," he answers. "I think it's time."

"Time for what?" I ask, thoroughly confused. My breathing shallows.

Toby steps closer, keeping his eyes affixed to my stomach.

"You need to remember."

"Remember what?"

"*I* need you to remember," he repeats, placing his hand upon mine, the one that is on my belly. His hand is warm and soft. Something about his touch calms my insides.

"Remember what?" I ask again.

His eyes roll upward to meet mine. "Remember."

Chapter 37

I scream and grip Jason's hand. He comforts me by wiping the sweat from my forehead. He leans in, getting close to my ear.

"You're doing great, honey. You're almost there. Just a little bit more."

The doctor peeks up from under the gown, "Okay, just one more push."

I hear the words and tighten, constricting my abdomen. My muscles burn from the strain. Jason kisses my cheek as tears leak from the corners of my eyes. I clench my teeth and groan, my chin buried into my chest. And then, relief washes over me. My muscles relax, and my head slumps back onto the pillow. My motion elicits an anxious response from Jason as he tilts his head sideways to watch the doctor hand our baby to a nurse beside him. I see the nurse's concerned look and squeeze Jason's hand. The doctor places two clamps onto the umbilical. He doesn't ask either of us if we'd like to cut the cord. He snips, and the nurse immediately turns away with my baby.

I don't hear crying. My lips begin to quiver as I look to Jason for answers, as if he knows something I don't. His face is fearful.

"Wh-what's wrong with my baby?" I mumble. "What's wrong with my little girl?"

The nurse looks over her shoulder at me for a second, remorseful, as the doctor slides in closer to her to inspect the baby. I can't see her. My thoughts spiral, and my eyes tear up. Why won't they show her to me?

"Jason?" I question, my words angst-ridden.

"I-I don't know," he answers. His frightened eyes are like nothing I've seen from him before, which only heightens my own anxiety.

"My baby girl," I yell out in both fear and anger. "What's wrong with my baby girl?"

And then a sound that echoes off the walls straight into my soul. A baby's cries.

I let out a relieved breath as my shoulders release built-up tension. The nurse turns and smiles, holding my swaddled baby in her arms. She apologizes for the terrifying minute that felt like hours to me.

Jason quickly wipes his eyes with his sleeve as tears roll down my cheeks.

"My baby," I say, holding my arms out to receive her. "My precious baby girl."

The nurse lets her eyes drift to the doctor and then back to mine as she places the baby on my chest.

"Congratulations, Miss Fitzgerald," she says. "You have a healthy baby boy."

A lump forms in my throat. "A boy?"

"That's right. He's beautiful."

Jason and I wanted the baby's sex to be a surprise, but I always felt like I was carrying a little girl. I'm shocked, but I'm ecstatic. We have a little boy. The proud father tears up, no longer interested in hiding his joy. Jason leans in and gives me a tender kiss.

"You did it, babe. You did it."

"*We* did it," I reply, smiling at his proud expression as he stares at our son.

"We'll leave you two for a moment," the doctor says.

As they pass by my view and exit the door, I see someone else in the room with us, quietly sitting in the corner. It's a young man, handsome, with short brown hair. He's wearing a bright orange vest. I recognize him from somewhere. I hear a distant echo.

You're safe now.

I blink, and the young man is no longer there, but in his place, a middle-aged officer sits and smiles at me. On his right chest, the name J. Cartledge is embroidered into the cloth. Across from his name, on his left chest, is a gold-embroidered badge with the word "Chief" on it.

It's me, John.

My eyebrows tuck. I turn to Jason in confusion, but he is distracted, completely engaged with our baby boy as he gently rubs his index finger along our son's forehead. I look back at the corner to find an old man now occupying the chair. He waves at me. I recognize him and politely wiggle my fingers.

Everything will be all right.

Then, a nurse walks back in. It's not the same nurse who was here before. She's wearing a different uniform. She steps in front of me, blocking my view of the corner. I lean to the side to look around her. She notices my effort and swivels sideways to see what has my interest. We both glimpse an empty chair. My shoulders slump.

"I brought you some Jell-O, Marney," she says. "Your favorite."

I reach forward with shaky hands, dark veins protruding from my wrinkled skin. Purple bruises are bathed along the underside of my arms. They drop like lead to the bedside, unable to carry their own weight. My body is as heavy as my confused thoughts.

"I'll leave it here for you," the nurse says, placing the plastic cup of green gelatin on a tray before me. As she leaves, another visitor has taken their place on the chair in the corner. A familiar sound hits my ears.

Thump. Thump. Thump.

I smile. Toby is here.

"Toby, you've come," I say.

The boy's legs stop swinging, and he stands from the chair, somberly making his way to me. He places his hand on mine, and it warms my heart. Toby always makes me feel better.

"Is it time?" I ask.

"No," he replies. "I need you to remember."

"I don't want to remember," I say.

He rubs a finger along the thickest vein on the back of my hand like he's following a trail on a map.

"Is it because of the pain?" he asks.

I turn my head away to look at something more promising, something that makes me happy, but Jason and my son aren't there. They've disappeared.

"Where's Jason?" I ask, turning back to the boy. "Where's my son?"

"They're not here."

"Where did they go?"

"Will you remember now?" Toby asks.

"I told you, I don't want to remember."

"But I need you to."

"I don't want to."

Toby's eyes shift to the window. "I'm sorry."

"Sorry?" I question. "Sorry for what?"

He turns his eyes back to me, but there is no tenderness in them anymore. Something dark within them stirs.

"This is going to hurt."

Chapter 38

"Run, Marney! Run!"

The words hit me like a freight train. It's my only chance to get away. But I can't leave him.

Through the driver's side window, I see Jason shove the first man just as the second man is rounding the front bumper to my side. I hear Jason scream through clenched teeth, "You're not going to touch her, you son of a bitch." A punch is thrown. The man coming for me stops and reverses direction. His friend needs help. Jason's words reverberate in my skull like a nagging itch. *Run, Marney! Run!*

I pull on the latch and shove the door open, almost falling from the passenger side. I manage to get my feet under me, and I take off for the treeline. A painful cry leaves Jason's lips, and I feel it in my gut. I hear the first man yell out, "I've got this; get the girl!" Adrenaline shoots through my veins as I near the forest, running for no particular destination-just away. I hear a cracking sound, and then a thump, like someone's body hitting the car. Footsteps from behind me are getting closer. I weave through the brush, tall grass tangling my ankles. I reach for something in my pockets, anything to use as a weapon. I pull out only the crumpled grocery list, which falls from my hand and cuts through the wind, landing on the hard ground.

I make it to the edge of the forest when something hits me. I hear the thud, but the world resumes. At least for two more steps before my knees buckle. A searing pain bursts from the back of my skull and travels down my spine like a current of electricity. The scenery begins to blur and fade.

I hit the ground hard, and a strange thought enters my head. I've failed him.

A hand grabs under my arm and yanks me up, almost pulling my shoulder from its socket. A second hand, rough and calloused, clamps onto the back of my neck. I'm escorted from the woods, mostly dragged, my feet scraping across the ground. My eyes catch sight of the car. The first man is standing on the far side of it. I don't see Jason. The man raises his fist and sends it crashing down. I hear the cracking of knuckles against cheek and know where Jason is. The second man, holding me in an iron grip, shoves me onward, forcing me around the car into the road, forcing me to look at Jason.

His face is bloody. The red liquid, mingled with saliva, drips from his chin onto his shirt. I shout his name.

"Jason!"

He doesn't respond, but the man holding me slams the heel of his fist into the side of my head.

"Hold her there," the man standing over Jason says. "I want her to get a good look at this in case she gets any wild ideas."

He walks away to retrieve something from his truck, but my eyes are glued to Jason. I mumble something unintelligible even to me. I'd fall to the ground if it weren't for the brute holding me up. Get up, Jason. Please get up.

The first man returns, an evil smile on his face, and stands over Jason's helpless, beaten body.

"Do you want to know how fucking serious I am?" the man seethes. He raises his arm over his head, and I see a large monkey wrench clenched in his hand. My heart hits my stomach. Suddenly, everything around me halts to a standstill. Well, *almost* everything.

Jason turns his head to me, blood still trickling from the open wounds on his face. He smiles, his dimples filling with the red liquid.

"You know I love you, Marney," he says, his voice soft, calm. "I always have. I may forget things, but I couldn't forget you. I will *never* forget you. I will never forget what we had together. I will never forget our son. But, Marney.., I need you to remember."

I shake my head. "No. I can't."

"You can, honey. I need you to remember why we're here."

"I can't remember. I don't want to."

I feel a touch against my hand, and I look down to my right to notice Toby, with his striped shirt, denim overalls, barefeet, standing beside me. He's holding onto one of my fingers and staring at Jason's bloody body slumped against the side of the car.

"You don't have to look anymore," Toby tells me in his usual mellow tone. "You know how it ends."

"How it ends?" I question.

"I need you to remember where it began," he says.

"No, no, no," I state, shaking my head.

"It's okay," the boy assures me, squeezing my finger. "Everything will be better when you re-member."

"But I don't want to," I say.

"This moment won't go away," Toby says.

Behind me, reality resumes. Everything that was still comes to life. I hear the wrench cut through the air and crack against Jason's head. My body jerks at the sound.

I begin turning to glimpse what that bastard of a man has done to Jason, but Toby tugs on my arm.

"Don't look. You don't have to this time."

Another crack, and then another, each sharper in my ears than the last. The man's sick laughter crawls down my skin. Toby grips my hand and stares into my eyes. Something about his features settles me. The laughter behind me, the continual smashing of metal to flesh, softens until there is only silence.

"What do I need to do to make this stop?" I ask the young boy.

"You need to remember why you are here," he replies.

"But it hurts."

"I know," he says, gently intermingling his fingers with mine. "But you can't blame yourself. It wasn't your fault. That's why I need you to remember..,

"Mom."

Chapter 39

With a single word, like a rush, it all comes back to me. I'm standing in front of the police station, the weight of my shoulders pulling me down to the pavement. I can't breathe, the two-block sprint from the park burning my lungs, but I know I have to go inside. I climb the stairs, two at a time, anything to get me there faster.

An officer holds the door open for me as he exits. I should thank him, but I'm too frantic to find the words. A partitioned wall stands in front of me with an officer sitting behind a thick glass window. She swivels in her chair to greet me.

"Can I help you?" she asks.

She turns in such a way that the light coming in from the front door reflects off the little gold tag above her breast pocket. My eyes flutter. She notices the glare and moves slightly to her left. I catch the name: L. Poole.

"You've got to help me," I raise my voice hysterically. "He's gone, missing!"

"Slow down," the officer says. "Who's missing?"

"My son, Toby!" I yell, slamming my fist on the shelf outside the glass.

"All right, ma'am; I need you to calm down."

"Calm down? I can't calm down! My son is missing! Don't you understand?"

"How old is your son?"

"He's eight."

"Can you tell me where you last saw him?"

"In our apartment. He was playing in our apartment. I had to get ready for work. I couldn't have been in the shower for more than five minutes. When I came out, the apartment door was wide open, and he was gone."

"Could he have gone to a neighbor's?" Officer Poole asks.

"No! Everyone in the building knows my son. They would have contacted me. A man on the first floor said he thought he saw Toby getting into a car with my neighbor, Angie. When I tried her place to check on her, she didn't answer."

"Has your neighbor ever taken him before without telling you?"

"Of course not."

"Do you know where she might have taken him?"

"No, but the other day, she mentioned wanting to take Toby to the park with her daughter. I thought maybe they were there. It's only a block from the apartment, so I ran there to see if I could catch them."

"You ran there?" the officer asks.

"My boyfriend has my car; his truck is in the shop."

"Ma'am, can you tell me what your neighbor drives? I can have officers check the area."

"N-no," I stutter. "I mean, I never really paid attention to that. It's silver. It has a dent on the passenger side rear panel."

"And Angie's last name?" Officer Poole asks, writing everything down on a lined pad.

Images flash before me as I struggle to gather my thoughts. I recall a brass nameplate on her door, though I haven't seen it in a while, covered by that damn wreath of flowers. What was it? It comes to me.

"Larson," I scream out, excitedly.

"Okay, can you tell me what your son was wearing?"

"He had denim overalls on. Um...a black and white striped shirt."

"And can you describe your neighbor?"

"She isn't too tall, maybe five feet six. Straight blonde hair just past her shoulders. Blue eyes."

"Anything else?" the officer asks.

"No. Please, find my little boy."

"We'll do everything we can, Miss..."

"Fitzgerald. Marney Fitzgerald."

The officer gets on a radio and repeats much of what I just told her. When she finishes, she turns back to me.

"We've got officers out there looking for any car that meets that description. Meanwhile, where is your apartment? We'll need to know which units both you and your neighbor live in."

I tell her what she wants to know, my mind racing. I'm not sure what details I'm leaving out. I've never been so scared. She tells me to go back to the apartment and wait there, in case the boy is simply wandering around and comes back. I reluctantly do as she says, though I'd rather be out looking.

Hours pass. I called Jason's work. He was out at a supplier's. I left a message to have him call me as soon as he got back to the office.

The apartment is cold, empty. Everything seems smaller, like the walls are closing in on me. I pace the floor, stopping occasionally at the window to look out for Toby, as if he would be standing in the parking lot, waving up at me. I look at his favorite chair, where he would annoyingly bang his little heels against the front.

Thump. Thump. Thump.

I hate that sound, but I would give anything to hear it right now. Instead, I hear voices and thunderous stomping out in the hall. I open the door to see Officer Poole and another officer running in my direction. As they reach the corner, Poole says to me in a stern voice, "Close the door and stay in your apartment, Miss Fitzgerald."

I don't listen. I know this must be about my son. I stand in my doorway, watching everything unfold in slow motion.

"Angie Farrow," Poole yells out, banging on the door. "This is the police. We have a warrant. Open the door."

Farrow? My mind questions.

Seconds tick by with no response. She nods to the larger officer and steps aside. He reels back, raises his leg, and kicks the door open. The wreath of fake flowers falls from the door, exposing the brass nameplate hidden behind it. It reads Larson. Both officers rush in, guns drawn. My curiosity gets the best of me, and I begin to step into the hallway when a small hand grabs me and pulls me back in.

Toby stands before me. Not my happy, beautiful Toby, but the other, pale, somber one.

"Not yet," he says.

The door slams shut behind me, causing me to jump and look back. When I turn again to face the boy, he's gone.

Hours fade away. Or is it days? I finally got in touch with Jason. He came home distraught when I told him the news. He wanted to run out and scour the city, but I told him the police asked us to stay put. Neither of us has slept.

After they tore through Angie's apartment, Officer Poole informed me of Angie's prior record. The woman had done this before, in other states. She's used multiple aliases, including "Angie Larson." The police had contacted neighboring towns and jurisdictions to keep a watchful eye. They had her information. They knew who she was. They knew what she looked like. Poole was confident they'd find her and have our little boy back with us in no time.

The evening crawls on while Jason and I embrace, holding each other for support. We cry, we scream. Jason adds holes to the sheetrock walls with his fists. And then, the sound we prayed for.

Knock. Knock. Knock.

I spring to the door, my heart filled with anticipation. Jason bumps against me in his haste to beat me to it. I yank the door open, expecting to see Toby's cheerful face. Instead, Officer Pool and the same officer who kicked in Angie's door stand rigid, stoic. Officer Poole's lips quiver as she opens up.

"I'm so sorry. We were too late. We found his body."

Chapter 40

The couch feels softer today, less stiff. Everything is calm. It's a beautiful day. Sunlight shines in, clean and honey-colored, spilling through the window and painting the walls in long, diagonal slats. Jason is gone, a cherished memory still clinging to life in old photo albums and silly knick-knacks, such as the cow key chain he bought for me one birthday. Toby, my beautiful baby boy, is gone, too. I know that now. Yet a vacant shell of what he once was sits in his favorite lounge chair in front of the couch, gazing blankly at me through sullen eyes. I stare at him, afraid to close my eyes for fear of losing him, until they are dry and aflame, and I have no choice. I blink.

-◆-

The smell of antiseptic with a touch of lemon fills the air. The nurse smiles at me as she fluffs my pillow. The low, steady hum and rhythmic beeps of machinery fill the void between silences. She walks around the bed to open the curtains, and I see Toby sitting in the small wooden chair in the corner of the room. I wiggle my fingers at him, unable to lift the weight of my arm.

"It's a beautiful sunny day today, Miss Fitzgerald," the nurse tells me in her usual chipper tone. She pulls the curtain open, and the immediate splash of light fills my eyes, causing me to blink.

The apartment is quiet. Toby doesn't kick his legs against the front of the chair; he knows how much it bothers me. Instead, he slides forward to the front edge of the cushion, just enough so that his feet touch the floor, and tilts his head like a puppy.

"Do you remember now?" he asks.

"I do," I reply.

"All of it?"

"Yes. It's all with me now."

"It wasn't your fault."

"I should have locked the door."

"It wouldn't have mattered."

"She couldn't have come in and taken you."

"She would have knocked; I would have answered."

"No, I told you never to answer the door unless I was around."

Toby shrugs his shoulders like he's unsure if he would have obeyed that rule.

"I should have locked the door," I repeat, fighting to hold back tears.

"We never locked the door."

"And look what it cost me," I say angrily.

"Look what you've gained," he answers, looking around the room.

My eyes follow, watching framed pictures appear on the walls, stories of a life lived in joy and fondness. The man in the photos, the smiling face by my side during the hard times, during holidays, for companionship, has aged over the years, but he's been there for me. He's been my guiding light during my darkest times, the man whose love and friendship I cherish. A tear fills my eye, and I blink.

The white linens are soft against my skin. The sores under my arms are thankful for that. Toby quietly waits for the nurse to leave before he gets up from the chair. The wood creaks. He walks to my side and slides his hand under mine, raising it from the mattress and pressing it to his chest.

"He's a good man," Toby says.

"Your father?" I question.

"John," he replies. "I like him."

"Yes, he is a wonderful man."

Toby rubs his fingers along my hand and taps my ring finger.

"You never married."

"No. I couldn't ever get that close again. I made a promise to your father that no matter what happens, even if he should one day forget me, that I would always remember him. That I would always love him."

"But you love John, too."

"I do," I say with a smile. "Where is he?"

"He's coming."

"That's good to hear," I say. I blink.

"You look happy in the photos," Toby says.

"Yes, I was quite happy."

"Dad would have liked him."

"You think so?" I ask.

"He only ever wanted you to be happy."

"Your father was a sweet man. I've never loved anyone as much."

"And Dad loved you."

"I know."

"John loves you, too."

I smile. "I know that, too."

I look at the boy's apathetic face and so desperately want to see him smile. It doesn't come. I blink.

-◆-

"Why have you come to see me, Toby?" I ask. "Surely, there are other things you could be doing than to spend your time with a frail, old woman."

Machines hiss and buzz along the wall behind my head.

"Nothing more important," he replies.

"But this place is cold and sad. Wouldn't you rather be home?"

Toby remains silent, gently rubbing my hand.

"*I'd* rather be home," I add.

"You already are," he answers.

I exhale through my nose and turn my eyes to the ceiling tiles. Thoughts run rampant through my brain, and a tear escapes my eye and runs down my cheek.

"You can't change what happened," Toby says.

"No. But why did it have to happen at all? It was bad enough when I lost you. And then later, those men. What they did to me, to your father." I inhale, trying to catch my breath. "I shouldn't have run. I should have stayed and tried to help him."

"Dad wanted you to be safe."

"But I left him. It was my fault."

"It happened for a reason," Toby replies. "Everything has a purpose."

"And what was the purpose of what happened to me? To us?"

The next few seconds of silence hit like a brick wall before Toby speaks up.

"John."

I blink.

"Is it time?" I ask, anxiously tapping my fingers on the couch cushion.

Toby stands from the lounge chair and sits by my side, placing his hand on mine.

"Almost."

I smile at his warm touch.

"I've missed you so much," I tell him. "Your father and I both did. Nothing felt the same after you were gone."

"He never blamed you for what happened."

I don't respond. The room goes silent.

"I think I'm ready to go," I offer.

"Not yet," Toby answers.

"Why not?"

"Because you still blame yourself."

"It was *my* fault."

"It wasn't your fault."

"I left the door unlocked."

"It wasn't your fault."

"I didn't do everything I could to protect you."

"There was nothing you could do. Angie was going to get me sooner or later. But your love protected me and kept me warm even after she took me. Even after she ki..."

Before he can get the word out, I blink.

"John saved my life, you know," I say.

"You saved *his*," Toby answers.

"What do you mean?"

"You gave his life meaning. You were his light."

"He was mine."

"I know. That's why I like him."

"Is he coming today?" I ask.

"He's on his way."

"I hope he gets here soon."

My breathing becomes shallow. I look into Toby's eyes. He's here with me. I'm happy.

I blink.

"Why did I have to remember?" I ask.

"Because it happened. Because it's important."

"But why is it so important that I remember?"

"For him." Toby points to a picture on the end table. It's a picture of John, the older version of him, asleep on the lounge chair, his mouth open, and an open book resting on his chest. He'd been reading to me while I was lying on the couch, recovering from a nasty fever. I couldn't let the moment go to waste. I snapped a picture with my phone and had it printed out. He still laughs when he sees it.

"He saved my life," I mumble.

"I know," Toby replies. "That's why you needed to remember him. I was the reason you were there that day." He points at the picture again. "*He's* the reason you're here today."

My eyes well up. "I understand."

I hold both of Toby's hands in mine. "Can you forgive me for what happened?"

"Can you forgive yourself?" he asks.

His words bite into me. I think of my life before it happened. Jason was the love of my life. We were happy. We had a family. We were supposed to grow old together. Then, a knife cuts away the fabric of what should be, and shows me what is: my life after what happened.

The years were filled with happiness and contentment. There was love and laughter, friendship and joy. Togetherness. John kept me whole. He kept me alive. He was my protector. He was my friend, my everything. We grew old together. And if not for John, if not for what happened, my life would never have meant as much.

I nod. "I forgive myself."

The slightest hint of a smile forms on Toby's lips. At least, I want to believe it's a smile.

"It's time, then," he tells me, pulling his hands free from mine and standing from the couch.

"Will you be coming with me?" I ask.

"No, I can't. I have to go."

"Go where?"

He walks to the door, opens it, and looks over his shoulder at me. "Back."

Then, he steps through the door into the hallway and disappears, leaving the door open behind him, like the day I stepped from the shower to find him gone.

I have no more tears to shed. They left me long ago. Jason, Toby, they weren't all I had. I stand from the couch and look down at the picture of John in the chair. I kiss my first two fingers and tap them to the glass within the frame. I walk to the open door and peer down the hallway. The light in the hall is exceptionally bright today. I step through the door and disappear. The overhead fluorescent light flickers.

Blink.

In the bright, clean room, with its beeping and whirring machines, and the sun's warmth splashing in from the large windows, bathing across her still form, Marney's heavy hand slips from Toby's grasp and falls to the white linen sheets.

Chapter 41

John steps through the open doorway in time to witness the nurse wheeling the heart monitor from beside the bed. He knows what it means, and his heart sinks deeper into his chest. He was late today. Traffic. He lets out a sorrowful exhale, alerting the nurse to his presence.

"Oh, Mr. Cartledge. I didn't hear you come in. I-I'm so sorry. Marney...Miss Fitzgerald, she passed on about ten minutes ago."

He inflates his chest, taking in a breath, trying to hold back the tears. He takes off his flat cap. His thinning gray hair sprouts from his scalp due to the static electricity in the dry air. He presses his cap to his chest with one hand while the other smooths over his unruly strands.

"May I, uh..." A shaky finger points toward the bed.

"Of course," The nurse interjects. "I'll leave you alone; take all the time you need."

He dips his chin. "Thank you."

The nurse walks by him as he steps deeper into the room. She stops at the door before exiting.

"Mr. Cartledge?" she begins. "If you don't mind me saying, you've been an amazing friend to Miss Fitzgerald all these years."

The word "friend" hits his chest like a fist. He would have liked there to have been more between them.

"I don't think I've ever seen anyone so committed to visiting a loved one as you have been," she continues. "It seems like just about every day since I've been working here."

It *had* been every day. Not only over the past few years at the elderly care facility, but every day before that. Whether at her apartment or when he'd take her to dinner, or when they'd go for long strolls in the park, he'd visited her every day since they'd met.

"I made her a promise," John responds.

"Well, I'm glad there were at least some days she remembered you."

John nods, pulling up the wooden chair from the corner and placing it by Marney's bed. The nurse stays just long enough to watch him place his hand in the elderly woman's. He stares at the IV bag, its fluid no longer dripping. She used to tell him she hated watching the drips. He slumps his forehead to the mattress, feeling regret for not being there in her final moments. There were many days she didn't recognize him since Alzheimer's and dementia took hold. She couldn't recall who he was, even when he would tell her. He didn't care, as long as he was with her. He liked to think she would have remembered him today, though, the anniversary of when they'd met. It was a day that changed his life. It was the day she saved him.

Others would claim *he* was the hero, but he knows better. He could never be as heroic as she was, after everything she endured. It was so many years ago, but he remembers every detail of the hurt and anguish she'd been through. She'd told the story so many times, he could live the events as if he were seeing them through her eyes.

Through her eyes.

I try to show enthusiasm, fake a smile about this trip, but it doesn't feel right. I watch the cow dangle from the ignition as Jason fidgets with the radio. Why did I let him talk me into this? His words erupt in my skull.

Marney, you can't keep doing this. It's not healthy for you to stay cooped up in this apartment all the time. You've gotta stop blaming yourself for what happened. It wasn't your fault.

How could he say that? Our son is gone because I wasn't responsible enough to keep the damn door locked or to know who our neighbor really was. That will always be on me. I'm the worst mother in history, and I'll forever carry that burden of guilt.

I only told Jason I'd go because I love him too much to let our relationship crumble. We've been through too much to lose each other. I can learn to get past this, to pretend it's all behind me. I can do it for him.

John lifts his head from the bed and stares at the woman who had been his unknowing angel. He thought about telling her so many times what he was doing there that day, but he couldn't bring himself to add to her burdens. If he'd told her, she would have always worried for him. He didn't want that. He just wanted her love. And she gave him as much as she could for as long as she could. He'd wished for something more intimate, that they could have been closer, but he understood her reasons. Like him, she made a promise, and he wasn't going to push her to break that promise. After all, he was a nobody, and Jason had been her entire life.

"Hey, babe," Jason murmurs, waking me from a restful sleep. "How about some breakfast?"

I have to admit, these past two days have been better than I expected. I needed this. Jason knew that all along. He's so wonderful. The hikes here have been spectacular, and they've kept me level-headed and sane. The smell of the trees, the morning dew off the pines, it's so exhilarating. I've noticed a change in Jason, too. He bought us matching hats. I can't believe it. Jason, wearing a hat? I never thought I'd see the day. And now, breakfast in bed? He spoils me.

"Sure," I tell him, stretching my arms over my head. "That would be great."

"Okay, there's something I've gotta take care of first."

"What do you mean? What is there to do?"

"I just have to run out to the store to grab some things."

"What do we need?" I ask.

"He pulls a piece of paper from his pocket and reads it off to me.

"Milk.

Eggs.

Coffee.

Bread."

"So, basically, we need everything," I say, smirking.

"We have sugar," he replies, smiling, showing off his dimples, which light up the room.

I pull the blankets off me. "I'll go with you."

"It's okay," he says. "You stay and relax. I'll be back in just a little bit."

I snatch the grocery list from his hand. "I'm not letting you go alone. You'll forget I'm here and drive home without me."

"Oh, you're funny. I could never forget you, Marney." He kisses me more passionately in those ten seconds than he has in the past three years since Toby...

"Either way, I'm going with you."

John brushes Marney's long gray hair from her face. He always thought she was beautiful and wondered if he'd told her enough. If he had, it still would have never been enough.

His eyes drift to the window, the clear, blue sky reflecting off his light brown irises. It's a beautiful day, he thinks. Much like that day started before everything went to shit.

It's such a beautiful day. People here in Vermont are so friendly. The owner of that little country store, Mansfield's Market, gave us a discount on our food. He said we were the happiest-looking couple he'd seen all week. What a lovely man.

The drive on our way back to our little rented cottage is a peaceful one. Jason took a scenic route down an old country road that seemed scarcely traveled. No traffic. No noise. No problems. Just forest and sky. But then, the car begins to sputter.

"What's wrong?" I ask.

"I don't know," Jason replies. "All the dash lights kicked on, and it's hard to steer."

The car slows, then bucks ahead, like it's skipping gears. Jason pulls to the side of the road just as it stalls.

"Shit!" Jason says, slapping his palm on the steering wheel.

"It's okay," I assure him. "We're not in a rush. Someone will be along. We can get a tow."

Jason huffs in frustration, trying to start the car. His eyes dart to the rearview mirror.

"Someone's coming," he says.

"See, I told you."

"Maybe they can help."

He steps out and waves his arms like a distress signal. A rusted, light-blue pickup truck slows and pulls along side us. There's a business name painted on the side of it, "Jeffries' Junk Removal."

An older man, greasy-looking, covered in oil-stained clothes, steps from the vehicle and walks around to greet Jason.

"What you got going on here?" he asks.

"The car just died," Jason informs the man. "It was jerking quite a bit. It might be the transmission."

"It could be the serpentine belt," the man responds. "Mine snapped not too long ago. It cost me $347 to get 'er fixed."

"Um, yeah. Okay. Is there a place you recommend that can give us a tow?"

"Us?" the man questions.

"Yeah. My wife and I."

Did he just say wife? Was that an accident? Is that what this trip is about? Is he finally going to propose to me?

The greasy man ducks his head and looks in through the driver's side window. He smiles grotesquely, displaying more than a few missing teeth. He winks at me and rolls his tongue along his upper lip.

"Good morning to you, ma'am," he says.

Ma'am?

He stands back out of view, *thankfully*, and discusses an option.

"I'll tell you what?" he begins. "I've got some chains in the back. You put your car in neutral, and I can tow you to the nearest station."

"You'd do that?"

"For a twenty spot," he adds.

"Let me run it by my wife."

He said it again. He called me "wife."

Jason leans into the window, "What do you think, honey? Mr., uh," he turns his eyes to the name on the truck and then back to me, "Jeffries here is willing to pull us to the nearest station."

I shake my head. "That might be a little dangerous," I say. I don't tell him the real reason I'm against the idea, that Mr. Jeffries gives me the creeps.

"Are you sure?" he asks, hoping to sway my decision.

"Let's just have him call a tow truck," I respond.

Jason huffs and turns back to the man. "Thank you for the offer, but I think we'll wait for a tow truck. Do you think you could help us out and call for one?"

"Suit yourself," the man says. "I'll see what I can do. I've got a CB Radio in the truck." Then he pulls a business card from his jeans and hands it to Jason. "If you have any junk you need removed, give me a call."

The creepy man gets back into his truck and drives off.

Jason gets back into the car and gives me a frustrated glare.

"He was only charging us twenty dollars, you know."

"I don't care. You didn't see the way he looked at me. We probably would have ended up dead out here in the middle of nowhere."

Jason sighs. "I hope he's able to get us a tow."

A different nurse peeks into the doorway, "Can I get you something, Mr. Cartledge? Water or a coffee?"

He clears his throat to dispel his sadness while he speaks. "A water will be fine, thank you."

"I'll be right back with that," she replies.

John wipes his face with one hand and with the other, rubs his thumb back and forth along the top of Marney's hand. He thinks about the nightmares she'd shared with him and the countless more she didn't share. How many sleepless nights had she fought through after that day? How many times had she had to look over her shoulder?

Things could have been different. They should have been. She always blamed herself. Not only for her son's death, but for what happened that day. She should have listened to Jason. They should have accepted the old man's offer to tow them. She should have stayed at the cottage. If she had, none of it would have happened. But she was stubborn and had to go with him. She always believed it was because she was there that day.

The day those monsters arrived.

Chapter 42

The tow truck pulls up in front of our vehicle and comes to a stop. I see a bent arm hanging out of the passenger side window. The driver gets out and approaches our car. Jason steps out to greet him.

"Thank you for coming," Jason says. "I don't know what happened. It stalled, and I can't get it started."

The young man sees me through the windshield and bends slightly to see me through Jason's open window.

"Good morning, Miss," he says, flashing a kindly smile. "How are you doing today?"

He's quite good-looking. The name patch on his shirt says "Freddie," and I am instantly transported to my childhood, when my Uncle Freddie used to invite us all to his house on the Cape. I feel comforted.

"Current circumstances aside," I answer, "I'm doing great!"

"That's good to hear," he says. "We'll have you out of here in no time."

"Where's the nearest station?" Jason asks.

"We've got a place just a few miles up ahead." He points forward instead of from where they came. "Let me just get some paperwork from out of the truck, and then we'll get started."

"Okay, great."

I watch Freddie walk back and hop inside the truck. After a few minutes, he exits from the driver's side, and another man, with a larger build and wearing a maintenance uniform, exits from the passenger side. The large man steps in front of our car while Freddie nears Jason.

"So how does this work?" Jason asks. "Do we ride with you in your truck?"

Freddie glances at his large passenger and smiles.

"Well, you see, there's only enough room in the truck for one more passenger. Why don't we take your little lady with us to the shop, where she can wait for you, and we'll send another truck out here to pick you up."

"No, I don't think that's such a good idea," Jason says. "It's fine. You can call us a cab."

"It's a long way," Freddie retorts with a funny grin on his face. "What if a cab doesn't come? You wouldn't want to be stranded out here in the elements with no car. I think it'd be safer if the lady came for a ride."

"Uh, you know what," Jason begins, a hint of irritation in his voice, "I think we'll pass on the tow. Sorry for making you come out here for nothing."

"Oh, don't you worry, it wasn't for nothing," Freddie says, nodding to his large friend. "Get her ass out of there, Hank."

The large man rounds the bumper, and my heart pounds in my chest. I don't know what is happening. I hear scuffling out of the driver's side window as a struggle ensues, and then the words that send my heart and feet racing.

"Run, Marney! Run!"

"Your water, Mr. Cartledge."

He turns and politely stands as he accepts the paper cup from the young woman, who is maybe in her early twenties.

"My dad was on the force for a few years," she says, offering the old man a smile. "He always spoke highly of you."

"Well, that's very nice," John says, taking a sip, his quivering hand almost causing water to spill over the top. "You tell your dad I appreciate it."

"Will do."

She leaves him in peace to enjoy the quiet time, but his thoughts are restless. Anger builds in his gut, thinking of what those bastards put his Marney through.

I'm groggy, barely conscious. My body vibrates from the dirt road we're on. The smell of tobacco stings my nose while the large man beside me clanks the lid of his Zippo lighter open and closed. My hair feels wet. I know it's blood. Blood! Jason! His face. What Freddie did to his face...

I close my eyes, but it doesn't erase the memory. I feel them next to me, one on each side. I'm trapped, wedged so tight. I open my eyes to get a sense of where we're going, but also because I know I can't let myself fall asleep. We're off the main road, now. We're on a small path in the trees, barely wide enough for a vehicle.

In between puffs of smoke, I catch whiffs of wet leaves and pine. Up ahead, I see a small cabin, swallowed up among the trees, nothing else in sight. As we get closer, I see the number 4 dangling sideways from a piece of trim at the front corner. The truck comes to a stop.

The large passenger gets out and yanks my arm, dragging me out with him. I swing my other fist wildly at his hand, screaming.

"Let go of me! Get your hands off me!"

The man places his other large hand over my face and shoves me backward. My head, which is already aching from whatever he hit me with before, slams into the open passenger door. It closes; I fall. He grabs a clump of my hair and pulls me to my feet. He swings me around, facing away from him, and wraps his bulky arm around my neck in a light choke hold. Freddie comes nonchalantly strolling around the front of the truck and steps up to me, nose to nose, his cigarette breath cascading over my face.

"You better quit your struggling, you little bitch. Hank here," he taps his large friend on his upper arm, "he doesn't say much, but he's been known to snap people in two. You wouldn't want anything to happen to that pretty little face of yours, would you?"

I don't respond. I can't. Not verbally, anyway. My shaking body is the only response he gets.

"Now, let's get a better look at you," he says, stepping back a foot while his eyes travel up and down my body. "A little skinny for my tastes, but you'll do." His eyes shift over my head at the man holding me. "She looks better than the last one, doesn't she, Hank?"

He steps closer and places his hand on my left breast over my shirt. I close my eyes in disgust while he fondles and squeezes.

"Yeah, I think I can learn to like you, little kitty."

He steps back and nods to his grunt. I feel pressure as the arm around my neck constricts tighter. Then, nothing.

John reaches over to the small table beside Marney's bed to retrieve the photo album they'd frequently looked through together. Too often, she didn't know who or what she was looking at, but she enjoyed the pictures, nonetheless.

It's heavy today, he thinks, as he slides it onto his lap. It gets heavier every day for his weakening arms. He flips through some pages, looking through the years that have slipped by. He stops on a few to admire the vibrant, healthy woman Marney once was. The Marney he knew in the early years. He smiles at a picture from December 31st, 2003. They were together at the Tutter & Associates New Year's Eve party. Old Man Tutter took the picture as the clock struck midnight, just as Marney surprised John with a kiss. It was a wonderful evening. Marney was laid off a year later, when Jedidiah's son took over the company. She never found another job she cared for as much.

John traces his fingers over the images of her face. He looks at them with great fondness, the way her freckles painted her upper cheeks and splashed over the bridge of her nose, giving her creamy, white features just enough color. She never cared for her looks. "Too Irish," she'd say. John never saw anything but loveliness.

His thoughts shift elsewhere, to another time. He sighs, shaking his head, thinking again of how those awful men could have done such horrible things to this beautiful woman. He sees it all, just as Marney described it.

It's not the feeling of my toes hitting hard against each tread that wakes me, but the sound.

Thump. Thump. Thump.

It reminds me of what I've lost.

I'm being dragged down some old wooden stairs. I try to speak, but words fail me, coming out as mumbled gibberish. We reach the bottom. It's dark and cold. Dank. I glance around to spy the plain gray surroundings.

"Wh-where..."

My words stop short, as I haven't fully fought off unconsciousness.

"She's waking up," Hank says.

"Good," Freddie says. "I like them lively."

He grabs my arm with one hand while the other latches onto my cheeks, squeezing them until my lips are shaped like a fish's.

"Let's see how she tastes." He forces his tongue into my mouth and slathers it around while his friend laughs. I try to pull away, but in my weakened state, he holds me firm, making disgusting sucking noises over my lips as his tongue dances erratically across mine and along the insides of my cheeks.

He pulls back, making a suction noise as his tongue exits.

"God damn, you're a good kisser," he says excitedly. "It's almost a shame I gotta do this. Nighty-night." I see his fist torque back over his shoulder, and then it comes crashing into my face. I hear snickering as everything fades to black.

John flips another page in the album and glimpses his younger self. A grin breaks his lips. He remembers those days, still a young pup on the force. He wouldn't have made it further if not for Marney. He certainly would have never seen Chief. She stood by him through it all, as he stood by her. "My protector," she'd call him, whenever introducing him to any of her friends or whenever he would introduce her to his. Pangs of guilt would run through him each time. He didn't protect her at all. Not from the hurt she endured. Not from the trauma.

Not from *them*.

I'm bound. On the couch. Freddie and Hank aren't paying attention to me. They're watching a boxing match on television. A news banner scrolls across the bottom of the screen. "Man found beaten to death outside his car on Kelley Stand Road."

I turn my eyes away.

To death?

Jason's gone. Dead. I want to cry, but can't find the strength. Or maybe I won't allow the weakness. I won't let these scumbags have that part of me.

My eyes look down at myself. I'm wearing someone else's clothes. How did I get here? My mind reaches back, pulling memories from places I'd rather keep locked away. I was in a basement. Shackled. I couldn't get free. Freddie came down. He forced me to eat catfood, the son of a bitch. He was going to do more. I pissed my pants. Then...then I was here. They changed my clothes. Why would they have women's clothing?

My body squirms at the thought, and I try to feel something between my legs to know if they've violated me. The couch squeaks from my movements. The men turn at the sound.

"Look who decided to join the party," Freddie says. I can't keep my rage contained any longer, and the words erupt from somewhere primal.

"You killed him, you fucker! You fucking murderer! I hope you fucking die! You hear me? Fucking die!"

Hank grabs a hold of the rope holding me bound and tugs on a loose end, untying the knot. My legs flop down, and my shoulders feel release as my arms spring from behind me to my sides, still numb from being tied so tight. He slides the strap holding my head in place off my forehead and pulls me up to a seated position. I instinctively swing my palm between my legs and apply pressure to see if I feel any pain. I don't. Had I the strength, I would have swung at the large bruiser instead.

Freddie slaps me across the face. My body begins to fall sideways from the hit, but Hank jerks me back upright in time to feel a second slap. Blood trickles from my nose.

"You'd better watch your mouth," Freddie says, "or you're going to end up just like that faggoty piece of shit boyfriend of yours."

My lower lip quivers, wanting to shout more hatred, but I think better of it.

"So, you like to piss your pants, huh?" Freddie says through gritted teeth. He unzips his dirty jeans. "Well, I'll fix that, little kitty." He pulls out his penis and flops it around in his hand. I turn away, but Hank grabs my head and forces me to watch. Freddie begins rubbing his hand on himself, smiling grotesquely as he eyes my disdain. "You like that?" he questions. My scrunched face and disgusted glare answer for me. "Yeah, you like that. I can tell. You want it, don't you? You want to feel me fucking you. All in good time, kitty. But first, you need to be taught a lesson. You don't piss yourself when I'm trying to sample the merchandise." He grabs a plastic cup off the TV stand and flashes it to me. He then proceeds to relieve himself into it, filling it to almost overflowing. I feel my insides churn. He extends his arm forward. A drop of urine hangs from the tip of his penis and drips onto his zipper.

"Drink it," he says.

"Fuck you!" I reply, my teeth clenched.

Another slap stings my cheek.

"I said, drink it!"

"No!"

He flashes a shit-eating grin, then reaches an arm behind himself and pulls something tucked from the back of his pants. I catch sight of the revolver, and my heart crashes against my ribs. He presses the barrel of the gun to my forehead.

"And now?" he snarls.

Reluctantly, I grab the urine-filled cup.

Chapter 43

John closes the photo album and places it back on the table. There's nothing within those pages he doesn't already know. All of the good times are captured on shiny photo stock for all to see. But it's what they don't see that haunts his thoughts. Marney lived with every harsh memory. As much as she opened up to him, in the beginning, and in later years, he could only ever imagine what it was like for her, experiencing the nightmare in real time. There was nothing he could do but feel utterly helpless as she laid out the dark memories.

-◆-

My hands shake uncontrollably as I raise the cup to my lips a third time, the salty taste clinging to my tongue.

"That's right," Freddie says, relaxing the gun back to his side. "Drink it up. All of it."

He chuckles and slaps his buddy on the upper arm like this is all a fun game to them. I force down another sip, trying to keep from vomiting.

"Tastes good, doesn't it?" Freddie chirps, re-fastening the button on his pants. He tucks the gun back into the rear of his waistband, then fiddles with his zipper, trying to straighten himself. My mind races. I need to get out of here. The door is behind me. Hank is giggling, watching his friend struggle with his stuck zipper, his hand still gripped on my shoulder, holding me in place. I can't take another sip. When I finish, they're going to rape me. They're going to kill me.

Courage bubbles to the surface, and I react before my senses can talk me down from the ledge. I thrust my arms upward, splashing the remaining contents of the cup into Hank's face. Startled, he releases my shoulder, bringing his hands up to wipe his face. I jump from the couch and sprint to the door. I almost make it.

Fingers grab a clump of my hair, yanking my head back. Freddie's lips scrape against my left ear as he says to me, "You're lucky I haven't fucked you yet, or you'd be dead right now."

He shoves my head forward into an oval mir-ror by the front door. It shatters against my face. Glass crashes to the floor at my feet. I fall with it, feeling warm blood spill down from my forehead and into my eyes. I see red. Figuratively and literally. Beneath my hand, I feel a shard of glass. I grab it and clench it tightly in my palm just as Freddie yanks me up by the hair again. Hank comes storming over in a rage, and I feel something stab into my left side. My eyes dart open from the pain. A breath leaks from my lips as my eyes roll down to see Hank's hand pulling away from my side, a bloody knife along with it.

"You idiot!" Freddie yells at his friend. "Are you trying to kill her? I wasn't done with her. She's no good to us dead. I'm not fucking a goddamn corpse, you stupid piece of shit. Now we gotta do this quick and fuck her before she dies."

He pulls me into him, my side burning. I can feel blood streaming down my side, absorbing into the shirt. Freddie sticks out his tongue and licks the urine salt from my lips. I don't waste the opportunity. I snap my teeth forward and latch onto his tongue, biting as hard as I can. He lets out a wail before reeling back and punching me in the stomach. My teeth let go as I cough from the blow. He backs away, rubbing his tongue with his fingers, making sure it's still attached. Hank snorts.

"You bit me, you stupid bitch!" Freddie seethes with a new lisp as his tongue swells, bloody spit flying from his mouth. He lunges at me. The hand at my side squeezes the pointed fragment of mirror. I swing my arm forward. The glass pierces fabric and skin, cutting his thigh deep. He screams out as I frantically yank the shard back. Before Hank realizes why his friend yapped like a little dog, I thrust it at the larger man, plunging it into his chest. My hand slides across its edge, slicing me near to the bone. I don't scream. I'm stronger than these bastards.

My uninjured hand grabs for the knob and pulls. And for a moment, I'm free.

-◆-

John leans forward in his chair and gently kisses Marney on the forehead.

"I never regretted a day," he whispers. There were things he could have done differently in his life. Places he could have gone. People he could have met. He might have even had a family had he tried. Nothing was ever as important to him as visiting with Marney. First, out of some sense of moral obligation. Then later, out of want and desire. "Every day," he had told her. He kept his promise. How could he not? That's what you do when you love someone.

He sits back in his chair, reaches into his jacket pocket, and pulls out a small book. Its cover has a tear, and its pages are well-worn.

"Mind if I read to you, darling?"

He opens The Little Prince, one of her favorites, and begins to read from it. He speaks the words, but he can't hear himself; his thoughts are back on that day in the woods, how Marney fought so valiantly to stay alive.

-◆-

I run blindly into the forest. The number 4 pops into my head. I saw it on the corner of the cabin. The address. There must be a 1 through 3 somewhere. If I keep running, I'm bound to find another house.

Blood continues to spurt from my side. I tuck my elbow against the wound to slow the bleeding. Pain surges through me, keeping my ears sharp. I know they're after me. I heard their screams as they charged out the door. I have to keep going.

The leaves are slick, making it difficult to gain traction. Twigs snap and crunch underfoot with each step. I run and run, not knowing where I'm going. There are no other houses in sight. I'm lost. I continue running for what seems like an eternity, ignoring the pain that, with every step, ignites under my skin. I must have run far enough. I don't hear them. I look over my shoulder while my feet keep moving. Nothing. I look back in time to slam into a large limb. It takes me off my feet, and my back slams into the hard ground.

When I regain my senses, more pain kicks in, but it feels different. It's thinning, spreading across my body. I'm going numb. I'm tired. Weak. Bloody. And then I hear their voices.

Adrenaline surges, and I crawl to the only shelter I can find: a large oak tree to hide behind. Their voices become louder.

"Here, kitty, kitty. Come on out, you fucking bitch. We've got a little treat for you. It's something really special for what you did back there."

I hear them snicker.

"Now show yourself, you fucking twat whore."

I hug my knees to my chest and close my eyes. They won't see me. They won't see me. They won't...

"There you are, you troublesome, little bitch. Did you think we wouldn't find you?"

My eyes open to see Freddie glaring at me triumphantly. He raises his gun to my head. I hear the click of the hammer. Then...

Bang!

Chapter 44

John pauses for a moment to catch his breath. Reading to her used to be so easy, so natural. Now, he needs to take breaks between pages. He looks at Marney, knowing it's too much to hope she'd open her eyes and tell him how much she's enjoying the story. He never cared for it much, himself. He liked grittier tales - police procedurals and detective stories such as The Snowman or The Alphabet Killer. But there was another story he enjoyed, a fairy tale. It was one of tragedy and loss, of love and redemption, of hope and happiness, where a sad, bitter man met a princess who gave him purpose and saved his life. It didn't end in a happily ever after, but it was as close as one could get. And it all began so many years ago on that horrible day. He remembers it all.

-◆-

Bang!

My bullet ripped through the man's arm, causing him to drop his gun as he screamed out and dropped to one knee. I could see the woman propped against the tree, her face covered in blood. Her body jerked when my gun went off, so I knew she was still alive. I raced in their direction, weaving around trees. The larger man went to his friend's aid. The man I shot shoved the larger man to the side and reached for his gun. I stopped, put the scope to my eye, and yelled, "Don't do it!" He didn't listen. He raised his gun in my direction, and my finger twitched.

The shot echoed through the woods. A flock of crows erupted from a nearby treetop, taking flight to safety. The man's cheek exploded as the bullet entered through his jaw and exited from the back of his skull. His body dropped, almost like it melted into the landscape. The larger man took off running.

"Stop!" I yelled. Again, he didn't listen. They never do. I needed to get to the woman to ensure her safety. I couldn't take chase, but I couldn't let the man get away, either. I raised my rifle again, aiming for something less lethal. I fired, and the man collapsed, tumbling hard to the ground, his knee shattered. He wouldn't be going anywhere.

I slung the rifle over my shoulder and ran to the injured woman. I didn't want to think about what would have happened had I not heard the men yelling. It was only dumb luck. She was fortunate I was here, in these woods, and that it wasn't ten minutes later, or we'd both be dead.

Dead.

The thought strikes me differently than it had earlier that morning. I entered these woods with a single purpose in mind: to end it all. And why not? I had nothing left to live for. My father died when I was seven. My older brother was killed in Vietnam. I wanted to join the effort, but the war had ended by the time I was old enough to enlist, so I joined the police academy instead. I thought it would give me purpose. It only served to expose me to constant stress and trauma. My girlfriend ended our relationship after two years, telling me she couldn't handle my persistent complaints about the job. And then, last spring, my mother passed away from cancer. I had nobody else. My life was worthless. So I had made up my mind.

It was my day off. I told my buddies I was going hunting, up in Vermont, where I knew they wouldn't come looking. I wanted seclusion, someplace where I'd never be found. Somewhere deep in the woods would do. I'd made my peace. I was ready to leave this world. I loaded the rifle and placed it under my chin. And then the yelling caught my attention. The cop in me couldn't ignore it. I'm glad I didn't, or this woman would have shared my fate.

I dropped to my knees by her side. She was still alive. She had a nasty gash in her forehead, and her hand was badly cut. Her wrists had rope burns upon them. Then, I saw the growing blood stain at her side. I lifted her shirt to see a nasty hole, blood still gushing from it.

"Shit!" I said. Her side took precedence. I tapped my orange vest, feeling for anything I could use to stop the bleeding. I pulled a handkerchief from the pocket and rolled it like I was rolling a cigar. I lifted her shirt again. "Hey, hey," I said to get the woman's attention. "Stay with me. What's your name?"

She mumbled. "M-Marn. Marney."

"Nice to meet you, Marney. I'm John. I'm sorry to have to do this. It's going to hurt. Do you understand?"

She nodded.

I took a deep breath, let it out, then pressed the handkerchief into the hole, using my thumb to guide it deeper into the wound. Marney wailed and kicked her legs wildly. I think I said "sorry" a dozen times while I continued to feed the cloth into the hole.

"We've gotta get you out of here," I told her, looking around. I tapped my pockets again, realizing I'd left my radio in the car. There was no need for it where I was going, and I didn't want anyone tracking me. "Fuck!"

I looked over at the large man in the distance, flopping on the ground and squealing like a stuck pig. Where had he been running to? I looked back at Marney.

"Where did you come from?" I ask. "Which direction?"

She raised her arm and pointed behind her toward the wounded man. Good enough for me.

"Was there a vehicle there? Did you have a car?"

She nodded, and then, with a strained voice, said, "His." Her eyes went to the dead man.

Of course, I thought. I stepped over to the man with half his jaw missing and dug into his pockets. I pulled out a set of keys, then squatted by the woman. I wiped my sleeve across her face to wipe away the blood.

"I'm going to get you out of here. Everything is going to be all right. You're safe now."

She was getting weaker. I knew she couldn't stand. I reached underneath her and lifted her into my arms. She rested her head on my shoulder as I sprinted in the direction she'd pointed. I slowed as we approached the large man with the shattered knee.

"I've gotta put you down for a second," I told her. "Don't go running off on me." I smiled. I gently rested her on a smattering of leaves and turned to the screaming man as he cupped his knee with his hands. I couldn't take the risk he'd crawl away somewhere. I pulled the rifle from my shoulder, leered at him with a curled lip, and slammed the butt of the weapon into his head. Twice, just to make sure he was out. Or maybe to make me feel better.

"Okay," I said, picking Marney back up. "Let's go."

I continued to run, having no idea where or how far I needed to go. If I had to run to the next state, I would have. Marney mumbled near my ear.

"I'm going to die."

"I'm not going to let you die," I told her. "You're going to live."

"How do you know?" she whispered weakly.

"Because I'm going to visit you every day to see that you do."

"Promise?"

"I promise."

John closes the book and tucks it back into his jacket. He lets a tear escape his right eye as he squeezes Marney's hand. He'd gotten her into that tow truck that day and gotten her to the hospital. There was no way he was going to fail her. It was only afterward that he'd learned the horrible news about her boyfriend. And later still, when authorities swept in and uncovered the remains of seven women and two children, uncaringly disposed of in shallow graves only twenty feet from the rear door of the small cabin, all in various stages of decay. Six of the nine bodies were identified within the first week of the horrific discovery. At least three of those found dead had been missing for nearly five years. There could have been countless more had he not been there to put a stop to it. That would have been Marney.

John was twenty-eight when he met Marney in those woods in 1985. She was thirty-one. It felt like a lifetime ago. She'd lost the love of her life that day. She'd lost her son three years before. As he sat in the hospital that day, praying she'd make it through surgery, he vowed he wasn't going to lose *her*.

John kept the promise he'd made to her all those years ago. He visited her every day. First, in the hospital, then, when she was released, at her apartment. For hours, they'd chat. Sometimes, no words were needed. Just being in each other's company was enough. Over the years, they'd grown close. Closer than friends. They had a loving relationship, spending time together, but had never become intimate. Neither would allow it for different reasons. Still, he only wanted her to have the best life. Just as he'd had the best life possible. He got to spend it with the woman he fell in love with, his best friend. Marney was with him as he advanced through the ranks in the police force, eventually becoming Chief, and she was with him when he *retired* from the police force. But no matter what it was, good or bad, what was most important was that she was *with* him, as he cherished every moment he was with her.

With a heavy heart, John stands from the chair and eases the door of the bedside table open. Inside is a keychain of a cow saying, "I love moo."

Next to it, an envelope. She always kept it close to her. John once asked her why she kept it in the envelope. Her response: "He never asked."

John pulls the sealed envelope from the drawer and taps it to his palm. He slides his finger under the adhesive, tearing it open, then pours the contents into his wrinkled palm and nods.

He looks at the beautiful woman lying before him. She'd aged, as he had, but he never saw it. He clasps her hand, leans into her ear, and whispers, "Thanks for saving my life."

Then, he carefully slides the engagement ring onto her finger. He turns, and a lone tear travels down his cheek as he walks out of the room.

Epilogue

The air hums with quiet, the kind that has weight, like a held breath after someone finishes a song. Grass moves around my knees, soft and silver-green. When I reach down, the flowing blades are cool between my fingers. The field rolls outward, a wide plain under an afternoon sky. At the edge, there's a line of trees, the same ones that used to mark the far end of the park, where Jason and I would bring Toby.

Toby stands a few yards away and waves, his smile brighter than the sun. He's wearing his favorite denim overalls and a striped shirt, his bare feet and ankles showing grass stains. I smile and wave back. He yells out, "Hi, Mom." It feels like a word I haven't heard in decades. I want to hold it in both hands.

I wander over to my little boy and kneel next to him. He pounces into my arms in a loving embrace. "I knew you'd get here," he says.

"You did?"

I feel his head nod on my shoulder. "Uh-huh."

He pulls away, and a gentle breeze blows through his blonde hair.

"Where's your father?" I ask.

Toby extends his arm and points behind me. I look over my shoulder and see Jason standing in the open field, his back to me, tufts of dandelions at his feet. I take Toby's hand, and we stroll over to his father.

When we get there, Jason turns to me and smiles. The sun reflects off his cheeks, accentuating his dimples. He hands me a dandelion.

"I've missed you," he says.

"More than any words," I reply.

"I have something else for you," he tells me, reaching into his pants pocket. He pulls out a little diamond ring, holding it between his thumb and index finger.

"You know, I had this for a while," he says. "The timing never seemed right. I was going to ask you during our trip to Vermont."

"I had a feeling," I tell him.

"But then, things happened, and, well..."

"The police found it in your pocket," I reassure him.

"Anyway, I thought you should have it."

He touches my palm and lifts my hand. He slides the ring on my finger. My arms wrap around him, and I squeeze him like I never want to let him go. Toby tugs on my shirt, and I release Jason to give him my attention.

"Can we stay here awhile?" he murmurs.

I look at the cloudless blue sky and hear a faint whisper wash over me like a soothing summer breeze.

"Everything will be all right. You're safe now."

I turn my eyes back to Toby and smile, holding his little hand in mine.

"Yeah," I tell him. "I think so. We can stay as long as you'd like."

A LETTER FROM THE AUTHOR

Dear reader,

I hope you loved *The Disappearing* as much as I did. I started this wild ride in June of 2025, but got sidetracked with completing my book *Reaper House* in time for Halloween, and then a little collaborative project with 23 other authors called *Horror for the Holidays*. Once I shifted back in mid-October, it was full steam ahead. I've never written so many chapters so quickly.

Anyway, if you enjoyed the book, I'd be very grateful if you'd consider writing a review on Amazon, Goodreads, or any of your social media platforms. I love to hear what readers think, which helps me grow as an author, and it makes such a difference in helping new readers discover my books for the first time.

Check out my website at:

javo-publication.square.site

Where copies of all of my books (including signed copies) can be purchased. You can also find them on Amazon or ask your local bookstore to order them.

Thank you so much for your kind support!
Jeff

Enjoy these other great titles!

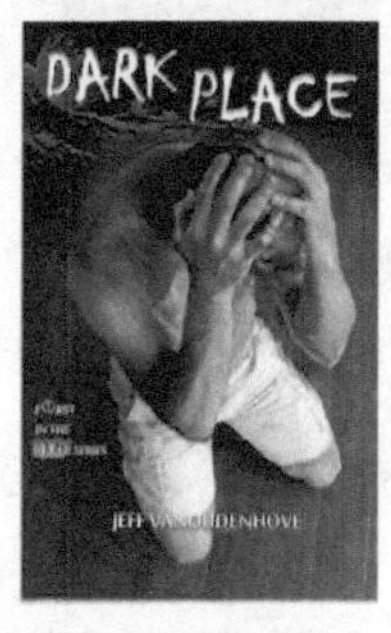

Acknowledgments

Hats off to my editor, Elizabeth Kelly, who does a fantastic job keeping me in line. I'd go into more detail, but she won't let me, which is fine, because there are so many others I need to thank.

I want to thank the members of the WhipCity Wordsmiths, who provided honest critiques and helpful feedback for some of the chapters in this story.

Thank you, Loni Wood, for the kind support and encouragement through the entire process.

I'd like to extend an incredible thanks to my very first ARC readers, Angeline Shipley, Brittany Hammes-Fox, and Cassandra Hoover, who have always shown such enthusiasm for my work.

I always try to showcase other authors and readers who have not only given my books a try but have helped spread the word through reviews or social media. In no particular order, thank you, Jamie Smith, Rachel Browning, Welz Bailey, Gail Clouse, Holly Smith, Kari L. Bowman, D.M Foley, John Randall, Daisy Carver, Dibbie Davis, Rebecca Yao, Carla Bradley, and so many more. If I missed you this time around, I apologize. I'll get you on the next.

Speaking of which...

On to the next.

Jeff VanOudenhove has written several novels in the genre of dark fiction, including the **Dark Series** (supernatural suspense), **The Alphabet Killer Series** (crime thriller), **Just Listen** (psychological suspense thriller), **Emma** (YA psychological thriller), **Screams in the Dark and Other Twisted Tales** (short story collection), and **Reaper House** (horror suspense). His talent for storytelling combines unforgettable characters and dire situations, mixed with astonishing plot twists. **The Disappearing** is Jeff's thirteenth book.